JERRY SCOTT a
JIM BORGMAN

ZiTS

CHILLAX

HARPER TEEN

An Imprint of HarperCollinsPublishers

Zits: Chillax
Copyright © 2013 by Jerry Scott and Jim Borgman
All rights reserved. Printed in the United States of America.
No part of this book may be used or reproduced in any manner whatsoever without
written permission except in the case of brief quotations embodied in critical articles
and reviews. For information address HarperCollins Children's Books, a division of
HarperCollins Publishers, 10 East 53rd Street, New York, NY 10022.
www.epicreads.com

Library of Congress catalog card number: 2013931374
ISBN 978-0-06-222851-2

Typography by Andrea Vandergrift
13 14 15 16 17   CG/RRDH   10 9 8 7 6 5 4 3 2 1
❖
First Edition

For Kim, Abbey, and Cady Lane

J. S.

For Joe Acito

J. B.

Our grateful acknowledgment to:
Phoebe Yeh, Jessica MacLeish, Tom Forget, Amy Ryan, Dan Lazar,
Rebecca Cox, Jeff Stahler, Ben Peters-Keirn, and Elaine Kaplan.

CHAPTER 1

I can see a bead of sweat clinging to Byczykowski's mustache hairs, and on her it doesn't look bad. Hector is right about Eastern European women being able to rock that look. He used to hang out with this chick named Autumn Solak, who was a total granolahead—meaning she never shaved her legs or anything. The first time I saw her in a tank top reaching up to get something off the top shelf of her locker, I thought she had two cats glued to her armpits. But she was really nice, and really hot, and Hector was crazy about her body hair. Personally, I'm not into that look, but I do admire a well-groomed mustache.

Every eye in the room is on the clock behind the teacher as it hangs on 3:29. And hangs . . . and hangs . . .

Ms. Byczykowski has this weird habit of overenunciating when she reads and accompanies that with exaggerated facial expressions. I guess she's trying to make sure we all understand what she's saying, but instead we all get distracted by watching the afternoon sun reflect off her gold crowns whenever she says "the Battle of Antietam." When she gets to the Emancipation Proclamation I'm going to have to wear sunglasses.

Somebody's cell phone vibrates, and thirty-five hands silently slide into thirty-five backpacks to check to see if it was theirs. It wasn't mine, and when I reach down to put my phone back, I notice a mouse-sized dust bunny rolling around under my desk. I watch it kind of randomly rock back and forth for a second, then rise slightly upward before it vaporizes from the wind force of thirty-five American History books simultaneously slamming shut.

It's 3:30 and the classroom doors burst open, creating hallway-wide rivers of humanity that roll through the building, around corners, and cascade down stairwells toward the outside doors.

Which is cool unless, like me, your last class happens to be on the first floor and your locker is on the third. I twist, spin, duck, and juke my way through the crowd until I finally make it to the first landing.

Pasting myself against the wall reduces drag as I gasp for air and watch the endless flow of studentage rush by. It's like standing on the edge of a freeway, only a lot more dangerous and about ten times louder. I'm serious. If you get near a group of cheerleaders on game day or in the vicinity of the Drama Club when one of them has a cute new pair of shoes, it can make your ears bleed.

Sensing a break in the flow, I dart in and hook my elbow around the metal handrail, and lowering my head, I push

upward through the crowd one determined step at a time. The key is not to lose hope. There's this story of a kid who did give up during a cross-grain stairway rush like this. They found tiny pieces of his backpack downstream in the metal shop and his shoes lodged under the vice principal's Prius.

I am not about to end up there, so I turn my focus inward and concentrate on my breathing as I fight against the current. Except for me the current isn't white water; it's elbows and saxophone cases and the enormous armloads of books carried by the simple freshmen who are either too insecure to use their lockers or too clueless to care about the hazard they present. Can't they see themselves? What is the advantage of carrying

everything you own everywhere you go? Is this a school or a refugee camp? As I turn the corner I drift farther toward the middle of the stream. Experience has taught me that this is the spot where the jocks hulk in the eddies and swat at the vulnerable with their bearlike paws, feeding on the weak and unfortunate.

And then suddenly the crowd is gone and I'm moving freely. The damp, Frito-scented air of the crowded stairwell has dissipated and been replaced by a cooler, fresher school smell of floor wax and urinal cakes. I've reached the third floor.

My locker is dead ahead, and I drag myself to it with my backpack and my dignity somehow still intact. All this just for the privilege of shedding a few eight-pound textbooks for the night. A stupid salmon who makes it all the way upstream at least gets to spawn. Lucky fish.

A few minutes later, I'm leaning against the van, talking to my friend Tim, when my girlfriend, Sara, and her best friend, D'ijon, come dancing out of school. They're singing this ancient Katy Perry song (Note to all girls: This never gets old), and after a final spin and a little butt thrust, Sara throws her arm around my neck and kisses me on the cheek. "Hi, Jeremy."

"Hey," I manage.

Let me just say this: Sara Toomey is hot. She's not Cheerleader Hot or Brazilian Supermodel Hot . . . she's more Ohio Hot. Perfect, okay, but not airbrushed and with just a few minor flaws to make her majorly interesting. She has this great smile (my dad was her orthodontist, so I guess I have him to partially thank for that) and a dancer's body that just moves in all the right directions at all the right times. But the best thing about Sara is the way she

talks. She's really, really smart, but she gets her words mixed up sometimes and comes up with more assaults on the English language than country music. Some of my recent favorites are:

I defy anyone to not fall in love with that.

I wipe the drool off my chin, and the four of us pile into the van. The girls scrunch way down in the back, afraid to be seen and ratted out to their parents. I guess they promised that they'd never ride in it for safety reasons or something, but I think it probably has as much to do with the lack of seat upholstery or possibly the exhaust fumes that waft up from the rusted floorboard under the front seat.

I finally find the key at the bottom of my backpack and wave my arm out the window to give the ignition signal. There's an electric snapping sound, a little yelp, and then the engine roars—okay, wheezes—to life. The passenger door flies

open and my amigo Hector Garcia hauls himself into shotgun.

"Hey," he says as he digs between the seat and the backrest for the seat belt.

"'Sup," I say, just because I feel chatty.

Hector is six foot six and pushing 230 pounds. We've been best friends since we were, like, four years old. We met on a dirt pile in front of the house that my mom and dad were building. That was where we discovered a common interest (dirt) and, even more important, that we were going to be in the same preschool class. It wasn't Best Friends at First Sight or anything with us. In fact, it wasn't until I bit Hector during a glue stick struggle and we had to spend an hour sharing our feelings about it with Miss Jenny that we became what you would call friends.

He rightfully bit me back after Miss Jenny let us go, making us even and launching an amigoship that's lasted all the way through elementary school and middle school.

We co-own the van, Hector and me, but he's the one who found a way to start the engine after the ignition switch got wonky. And he says that he hardly even feels the shocks anymore. However, I take credit for noticing that the wires on his retainer happen to be the perfect length for this operation. Since Hector always wears his retainer, he's the designated starter, and we're never without a van key. I'm happy, he's happy, and his orthodontist has a BMW.

Plus, the faint electrical-ozone tang on Hector's breath is an improvement over the smell of his grandma's habanero red sauce that he pours on almost everything he eats (I saw him put it on a bowl of Lucky Charms once, in case you think I'm exaggerating). The guy has a Kevlar stomach.

The van shudders forward like some kind of arctic Chihuahua as we inch along in the school parking lot traffic (I do the best I can, but we do need to get that clutch fixed). I don't know why the traffic is always so bad. You have maybe two or three hundred teen-age drivers who are all in an insane rush to get as far away from school as fast as possible. Could someone please explain it to me? The van rolls forward another quarter-tire revolution. We're moving slower than the line outside the women's restroom at a concert.

Speaking of concerts, Hector turns around and rests his meaty elbows on the back of the seat. He smiles at Sara and D'ijon as he scratches the little soul patch under his lower lip with two shiny Gingivitis passes. "I wonder if there's anybody we know who's cool enough to have actual tickets to the actual Gingivitis concert next weekend," he fake muses.

"OHMYGAWDICAN'TBELIEVEYOUGUYSGOTTICKETS," the girls scream.

The line of cars trying to get out of the school parking lot is endless, so we have plenty of time to really rub it in. So I say, "Gosh, if I knew you were interested, I would have gotten tickets for you— Oh, wait . . . you're the girls with curfews who always follow the rules."

"I am *so* jealous." Sara pouts as she grabs the tickets from Hector. She sniffs them and then starts rubbing them all over her neck. "Mmmmmm . . . ." she purrs. "I can almost smell the roadies!"

This is the effect that certain music has on females, and the main reason I have dedicated my life to rock music. It's common knowledge that the average rock star is up to 30 percent uglier than the average non–rock star, yet 900 percent more likely to be seen hanging out with supermodels. It's simple math.

D'ijon grabs the tickets from Sara and starts studying them like some kind of an exam guide before a midterm.

"Can you imagine what our parents would say if they saw us even *holding* these tickets?"

See, Gingivitis has a reputation for some pretty insane stage behavior. Sure, there has been the occasional wardrobe slippage, virgin sacrifice, and live animal ingestion, but it's not like these guys use that to get attention. They are first and foremost musicians. And people always bring this up, but I personally think the exploding-porpoise-bazooka thing never really happened and was just some story their publicist concocted to sell tickets . . . which is something that I can't believe they even need to worry about.

These guys are gods.

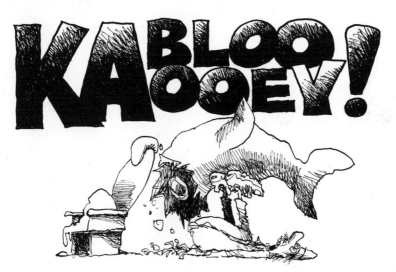

Their music is the basis for everything our band is and wants to be. Seriously, Gingivitis is arguably the best guitar mayhem band since Flatulent Rat, and that's not something I would say casually.

Anyway, we're all talking while Tim (who's always quiet normally) just sits there watching it all happen and texting somebody off and on.

I look at Hector and say pretty loudly, "Dude, what kind of loser sells tickets to a Gingivitis concert when he's not having brain surgery or something?"

And Hector goes, "Unfathomable, dude."

I make a smirking glance in the rearview mirror and see that Tim is still texting. The guy doesn't even look up during this barrage of dissitude. I mean, can you even imagine having two primo tickets to the biggest concert of the year and then letting them go because you have to do something with your *mom*? Seriously, dude. Get your priorities straight for once.

Then all at once a cheer goes up as I make the turn out of the parking lot. By second gear I've built up enough speed to outrun the cloud of oil smoke that we've been breathing for the past five minutes. I wonder if Hector's retainer could do a tune-up on the van, too?

CHAPTER 2

It's, like, one thirty a.m. and I'm thinking about getting started on my ethics paper that's due Monday: "Create a time line and discuss the historical significance of the Watergate scandal during the Nixon administration (1969–1974)." Yuh. That makes sense. Like I have time for writing a thousand words on something that happened, like, a billion years ago.

Wisely, I've spent most of the evening putting a killer history-paper-writing music playlist together that'll get me through this assignment . . . and it totally rocks. In fact, it's so good that I'm going to post it on my Facebook page. Here's what I have so far:

▲ Name	Time	Artist	Album
1 Kitten in the Woodchipper	5:42	Gingivitis	Does This Look Infected?
2 Scandalous (Live)	4:07	Flatulent Rat	Beans for Breakfast
3 Paranoid Freakazoid	6:12	The Busted Nixons	Nattering Nabobs
4 Rotten to the Core	4:53	Dumpster Fire	Dumpster Fire
5 Projectile Politics	3:24	Gingivitis	Spank Me
6 Too Many Crooks in the Kitchen	3:19	Trashpile	Essential Trashpile
7 History Never Happened	7:45	Gingivitis	Does This Look Infected?
8 Down in Flames (Remastered)	6:05	Flatulent Rat	Case o' Beano
9 Alleged Incident	4:19	Anxious Phlegm	Critical Earache
10 Hysterical Hypochondriacs	12:37	Spiro	Spiro Who?
11 Saturday Night Massacre	4:59	Roasted Toast	I Am Not a Cook

iTunes — Waterbed Playlist

This paper is practically going to write itself. I check a few other people's Facebooks, make a sandwich (I'm starving!), and start surfing for background on Nixon and his Waterbed scandal, whatever that was.

SLOSH! SLOSH! SLOSH! SLOSH!

My phone vibrates with about the millionth text from Hector tonight. We have been going back and forth all night about the concert. It's insane. We haven't been this jacked about something since, like, ever. Hector wants me to check out a YouTube link of Gingivitis on *Conan*, which I do. Hilarious, of course. Then I text him back an LOL along with this awkward question I've had on my mind for a while:

The guy has become obsessive about his looks, and I guess it's sort of rubbing off on me a little.

Ever since the three-girl posse of Redondo, LaJolla, and Zuma gave Hector a complete makeover—hairstyle, clothes, contacts— the guy has been looking much less gross than usual. We were standing around in the hall one day and

he was like, "Dude, I need some new clothes." And I was all, "Let's go. I'll help you buy some stuff." And the Posse goes, "YOU?? HA! HA! HA! HA! HA! HA!" Then they just dragged him off, and the next thing you know he shows up at school with a cool haircut, clothes that fit, and swarms of girls asking to touch the soul patch under his lower lip that he grew overnight. The dude can rock the facial hair.

I would ordinarily never ask another guy what he's wearing anyplace, except that whatever Hector is doing, it's working.

And I really don't want to look like a total tool at my first concert.

Correction: Gingivitis won't be my *first* concert. When I was in middle school, my grandma got me tickets for this pretty desperate Christian rock group called Serpent Slappers that was playing in the Lutheran church Youth Hall (read: basement). My mom and dad drove me there and proceeded to stay for the show, standing in the doorway and swaying to some of the slow songs. Then when the band got to their heavier stuff my mom started doing that chicken thing with her neck and snapping her fingers, and my dad . . . my dad was worse. Let me just say that the words *dad* and *pelvic thrusts* should never be used in the same sentence, okay? At some point, somebody in the crowd noticed him, and I sank down in my seat so fast that I got third-degree Naugahyde burns on the back of my neck.

The cool thing is that the incredibleness of the Gingivitis concert will definitely erase the humiliation I still feel every time I drive by that church or my mom plays her *Awesome Funky Savior* CD that she bought after the show.

My phone rings and it's Hector, of course. "Dude! I have a total blueprint of the concert logistics," he says. "Everything is nailed down, including a GPS map of the parking space for the van and an algorithm for estimating how long we can party with the band after we get backstage and still not break curfew."

You gotta respect a guy who can go full nerd *and* be cool enough to kick back with Gingivitis. The only minor problem we still have to solve is that we don't technically have permission from our parents to go to the concert. Ever since the Cricket Incident last week at school, we've both been lying low. Okay, we're grounded.

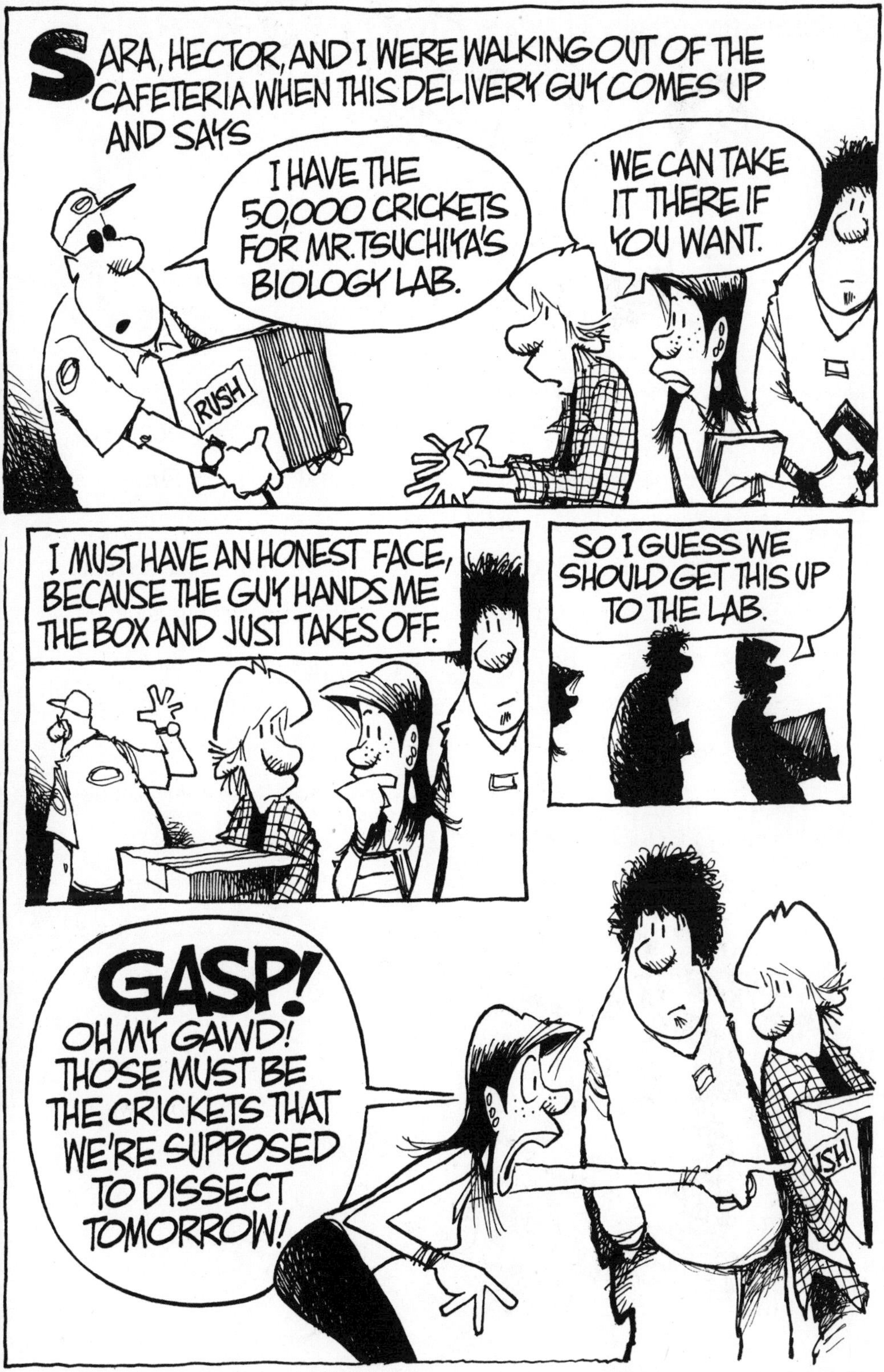
SARA, HECTOR, AND I WERE WALKING OUT OF THE CAFETERIA WHEN THIS DELIVERY GUY COMES UP AND SAYS
I HAVE THE 50,000 CRICKETS FOR MR. TSUCHIYA'S BIOLOGY LAB.
RUSH
WE CAN TAKE IT THERE IF YOU WANT.
I MUST HAVE AN HONEST FACE, BECAUSE THE GUY HANDS ME THE BOX AND JUST TAKES OFF.
SO I GUESS WE SHOULD GET THIS UP TO THE LAB.
GASP!
OH MY GAWD! THOSE MUST BE THE CRICKETS THAT WE'RE SUPPOSED TO DISSECT TOMORROW!
USH

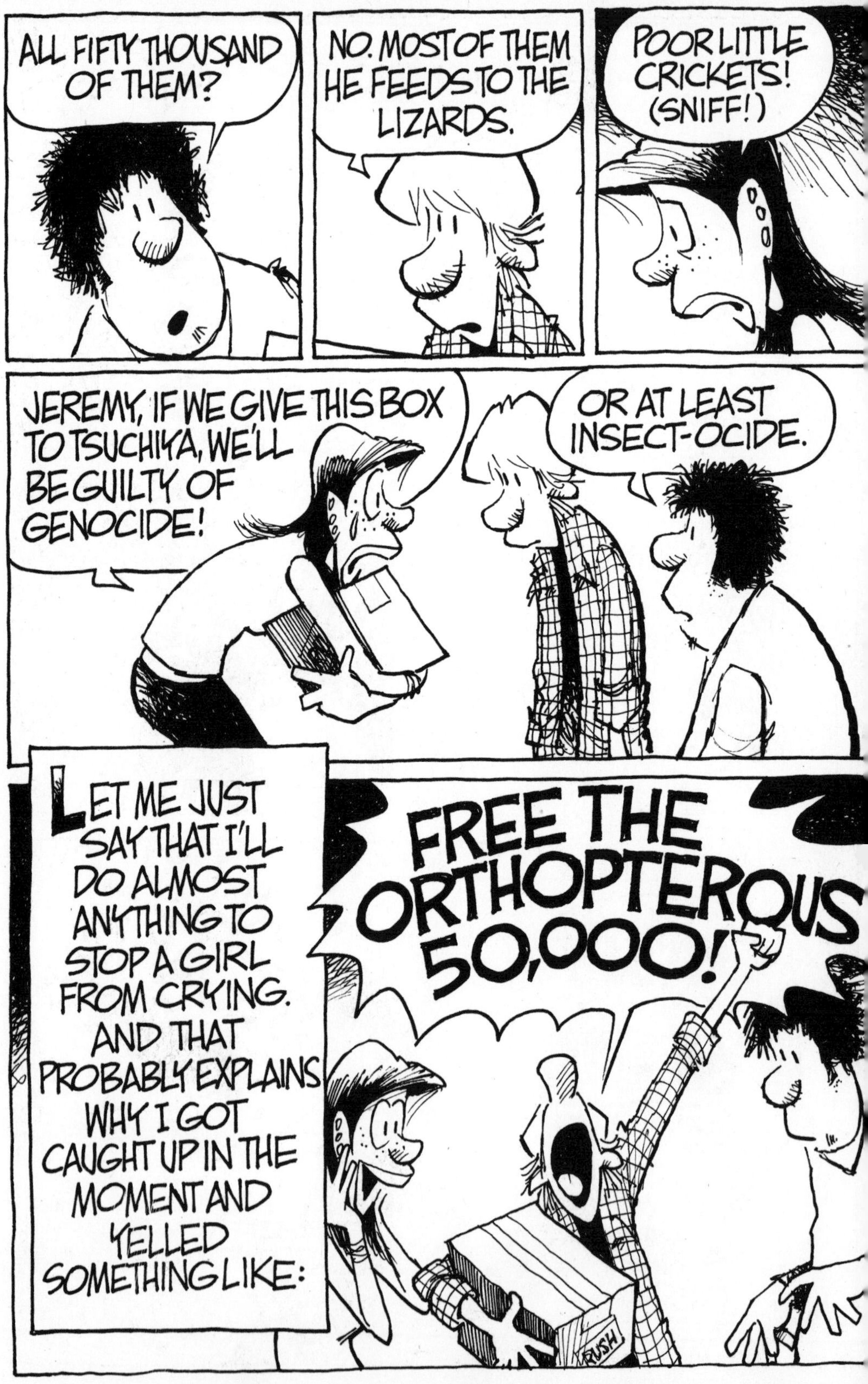
ALL FIFTY THOUSAND OF THEM?
NO. MOST OF THEM HE FEEDS TO THE LIZARDS.
POOR LITTLE CRICKETS! (SNIFF!)
JEREMY, IF WE GIVE THIS BOX TO TSUCHIYA, WE'LL BE GUILTY OF GENOCIDE!
OR AT LEAST INSECT-OCIDE.
LET ME JUST SAY THAT I'LL DO ALMOST ANYTHING TO STOP A GIRL FROM CRYING. AND THAT PROBABLY EXPLAINS WHY I GOT CAUGHT UP IN THE MOMENT AND YELLED SOMETHING LIKE:
FREE THE ORTHOPTEROUS 50,000!
RUSH

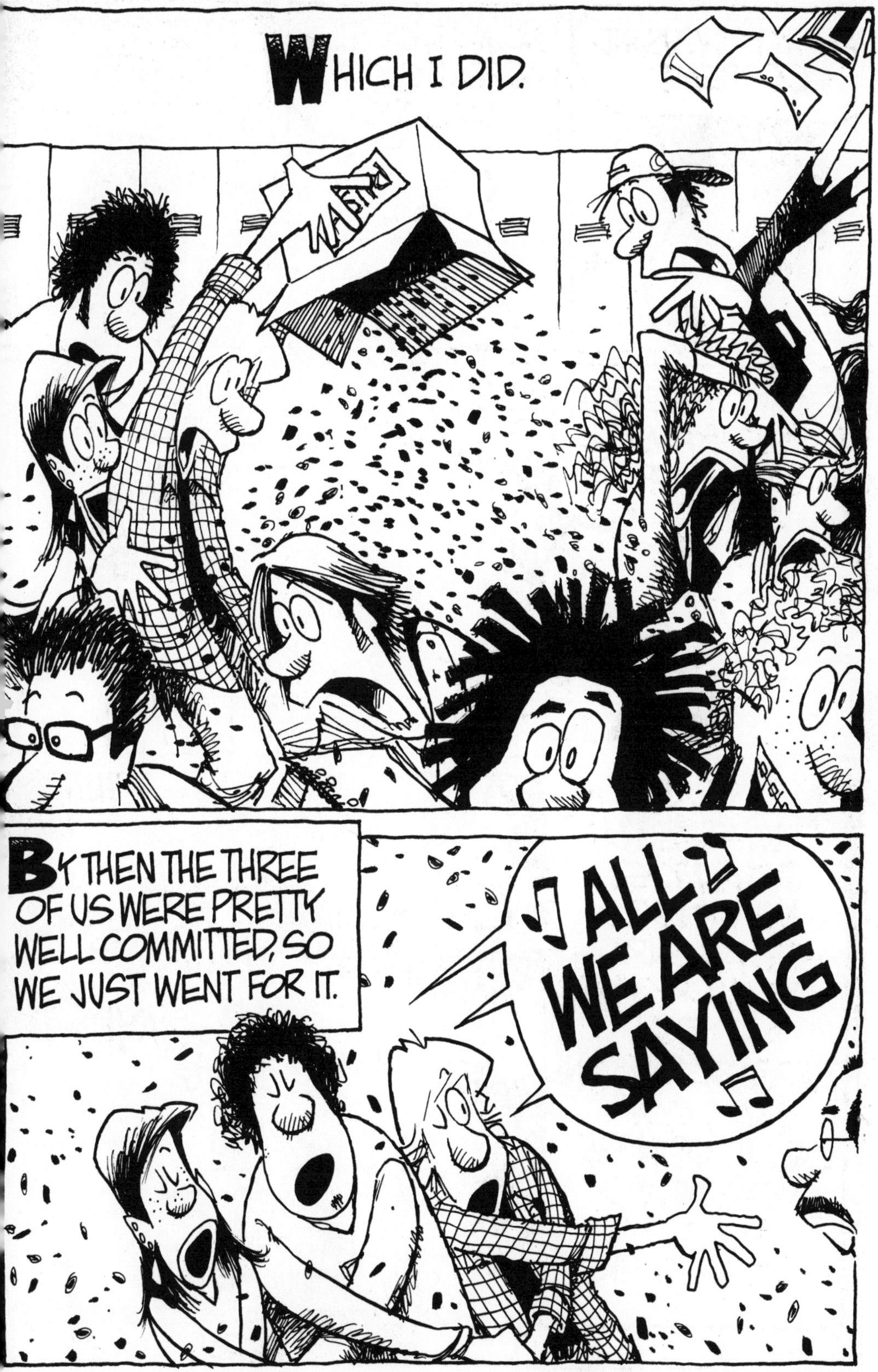
WHICH I DID.
BY THEN THE THREE OF US WERE PRETTY WELL COMMITTED, SO WE JUST WENT FOR IT.
ALL WE ARE SAYING

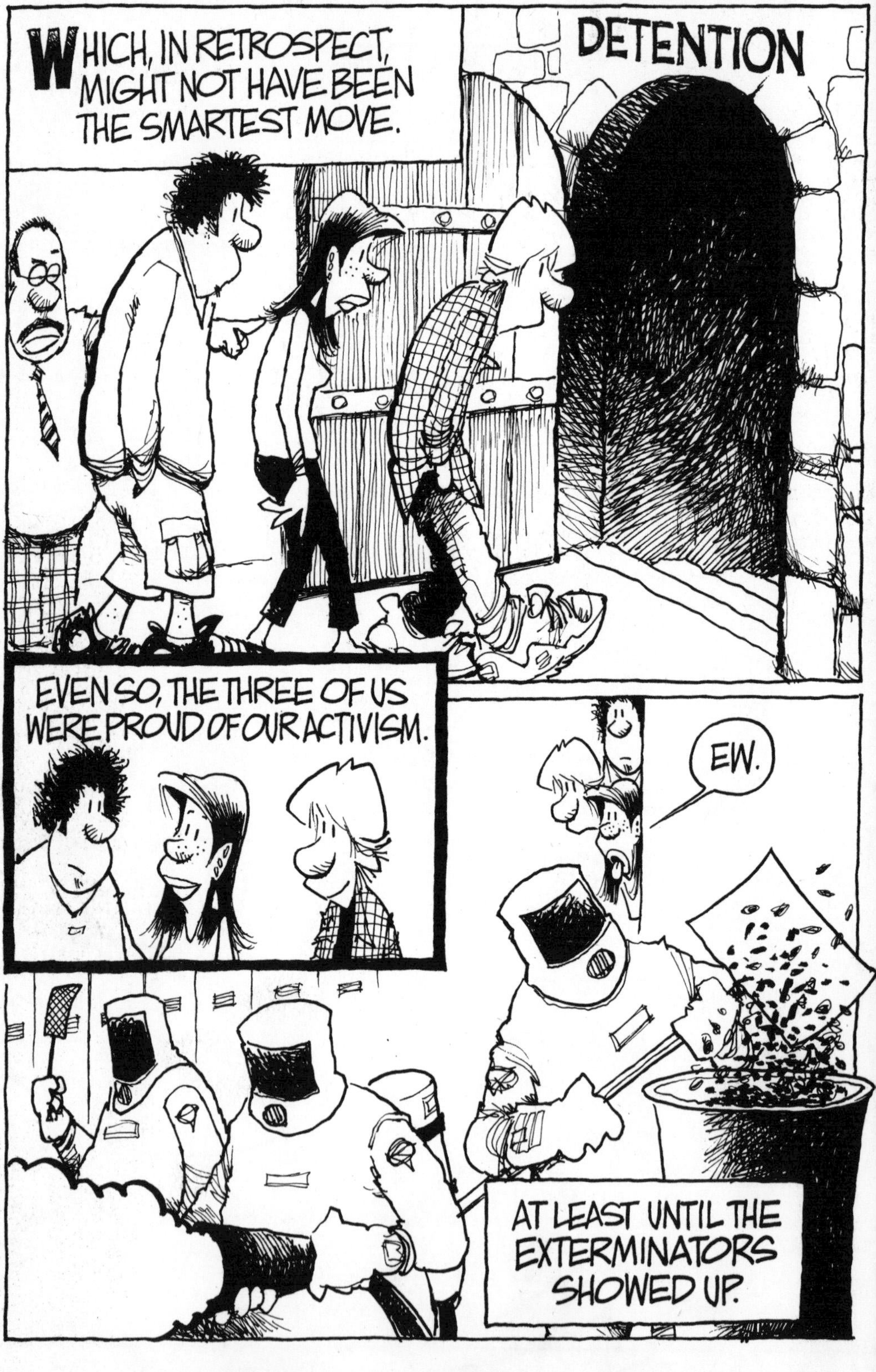
WHICH, IN RETROSPECT, MIGHT NOT HAVE BEEN THE SMARTEST MOVE.
DETENTION
EVEN SO, THE THREE OF US WERE PROUD OF OUR ACTIVISM.
EW.
AT LEAST UNTIL THE EXTERMINATORS SHOWED UP.

Whatever. Detention wasn't that bad (Sara was there, too), and I don't really mind being grounded because I don't mind spending time alone in my room. Why do parents consider that punishment, anyway? Half the time they're trying to pry me *out* of my room, and then when I screw up and get in trouble, they turn around and send me back in there, which is where I wanted to be in the first place! If you ask me, the only real punishment in the world is anything that falls under the heading of "Fun for the Whole Family," which, trust me, is a lie.

Aside from the obvious crap I have to put up with, my parents are actually pretty cool. It's just unfortunate for me that they both chose careers that would put them in direct contact with my friends once I became a teenager. My dad is an orthodontist, and my mom is a child psychologist specializing in adolescent weirdism, I think. She hasn't really worked since I came along.

OH, RIGHT!

The woman says that she's writing a book called *My Teenager Ate My Brain* (hilarious, Mom). Every time something happens, like I forget to turn the shower off for a week or back her car up the side of the house (not my fault—it was foggy that morning), she jets off to her bedroom office and starts wailing away on her laptop, solving problems for the future parents of future teenagers. Yeah, good luck with that, Mr. and Mrs. Doomed-to-Failure.

And because she's a "professional," she considers it her job to wring every particle of emotion out of me she can possibly get her hands on.

HOW DOES THAT MAKE YOU FEEL?

There it is, her *F* word. Feelings. Everything is about feelings with my mom. She just doesn't get it that guys don't *have* feelings.

But it evens out, since my dad is, like, the polar opposite of my mom, communication-wise. His yin can go toe-to-toe with her yang any day. Where one of my mom's lectures can last longer than a Peter Jackson movie, my dad usually gets his point across with a simple "Stop being an idiot." After a full day of tightening braces and realigning jawbones, the last thing he wants to do is deal with more teenage drama.

You wouldn't think it by looking at him, but he's actually

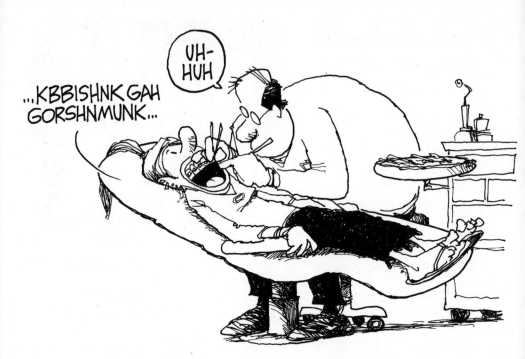

pretty sharp, which is why I have to handle this getting permission thing very carefully. I can usually get my mom to agree to anything if I make eye contact with her while I'm begging, but my dad is less susceptible to that kind of stuff. And he does his research. I know this guy in my geometry class who had to sell his concert tickets after his parents read a Wikipedia entry about Gingivitis's spotty record of, um, let's call it role modeling. That's exactly the kind of thing my dad would do, so just to cover my bases, I've taken down their poster in my room, blocked all references to the band on our computers and renamed any playlists featuring Gingivitis "Easy Listening." If I'm going to get to this concert, I'm going to have to fake sincerity on a whole new level.

"Did you ask your parents if you could go to the concert yet?" I ask Hector.

"Sort of," he says. "I'm working up to it. What about you?"

Hector operates under the mistaken assumption that responsible behavior results in increased freedoms. Uh-huh. That might work for him, but in my experience, helping out around the house only earns me more chores and unwanted attention from my parents. I prefer a more classic approach to getting my way.

"Not yet," I say. "Hey, have you started on that ethics paper?"

"Yeah. Like last week. I handed it in three days ago. Are you still working on yours?" I hate it when he does this, and he does it all the time. He finishes his homework on the day it's assigned and turns it in the day it's due. I wouldn't be surprised if the dude has even read a syllabus. This kind of irresponsible competency has consequences . . . like making me look bad.

"Almost. I've been waiting for the motivation to kick in."

"What motivation is that?" he asks.

CHAPTER 3

I woke up this morning, did my stuff, got dressed, and went downstairs.

As usual, my parents were already on my case.

I stifle my comeback because (a) I only got nine hours of

sleep, and (b) I'm technically still grounded and need to make a few deposits into my good karma bank. It's all part of the way things work around here. I make a small error in judgment, and then I act all helpful and nice for a few days until the heat blows over. One example might be the time I texted a couple of people that my parents might be going out of town and I might be having a party (I'm pretty sure I said "might"). Three hundred nineteen random teenagers, four squad cars, and seven finger-pointing neighbors later, I was grounded. It took me almost two weeks of *Yes, Dad*s and *Sure, Mom*s, but eventually my mom's mouth lost that permafrown and my dad could look the neighbors in the eye again. It's funny. I seem to get over these things a lot faster than either of my parents does. If it weren't for my sunny outlook and my huge capacity for self-forgiveness, they might stay mad forever. It's another one of the many things I contribute to the family. Without that, they'd probably have bars bolted over my bedroom window and be feeding me through a slot in the door by now.

So I focus on the cereal in my bowl like a Jedi master and use my powers to levitate it directly into my mouth. When it doesn't work I shift my concentration to the milk carton across the table and try to bring it to my hand.

After about forty-five seconds of watching this, my mom says, "Oh, for Pete's sake!" and hands it to me. My powers are definitely growing.

I adjust the angle of my laptop so my mom

won't see the Gingivitis video I'm watching. I've studied this thing, like, a thousand times this week. The guys are playing an absolutely unconscious version of "Quintuple Amputee." I shove my earbuds in a little tighter so my mom can't hear, push Play again, keeping my finger on the Esc key, just in case she looks over this way. Nigel Mealsworth plays this insane chord that doesn't even have a name and is so difficult to form that it's rumored to have been outlawed in several southern states. I'm determined to master the heart of the song, but it flashes by like a hummingbird on Red Bull. No matter how many times I pause it, I just catch a blur. As I scrub back and forth one frame at a time, a passing shadow dims the iridescence of my Fruit Loops, distracting me, and I miss it again.

"Hi, Hector," says my mom.

"Hey, Mrs. D.," (he never calls her Mrs. Duncan), and that explains the shadow across my screen. Hector knows where we hide our house key, so he generally lets himself in rather than bothering us to get up to answer the door. He claims that he can list that as community service on his college application someday.

Mom pulls out the emergency backup cereal

box, and Hector opens it and drains it into a bowl. I look over at Hector and say, “This is another thing I don’t get. Why do they make cereal so delicious and cereal bowls so small?”

The crunching coming from Hector is really loud, but he’s nodding, so I raise my voice a little and continue. “It doesn’t make any sense to me. When you wake up hungry, there’s no substitute for a salad bowl and a sturdy ladle for uploading some serious nutrition.”

“Mfngndl,” Hector replies, so I pass him the hot sauce.

Band practice is in my garage today, which means I have to suffer through the worst torture on earth: My Parents Talking to My Friends.

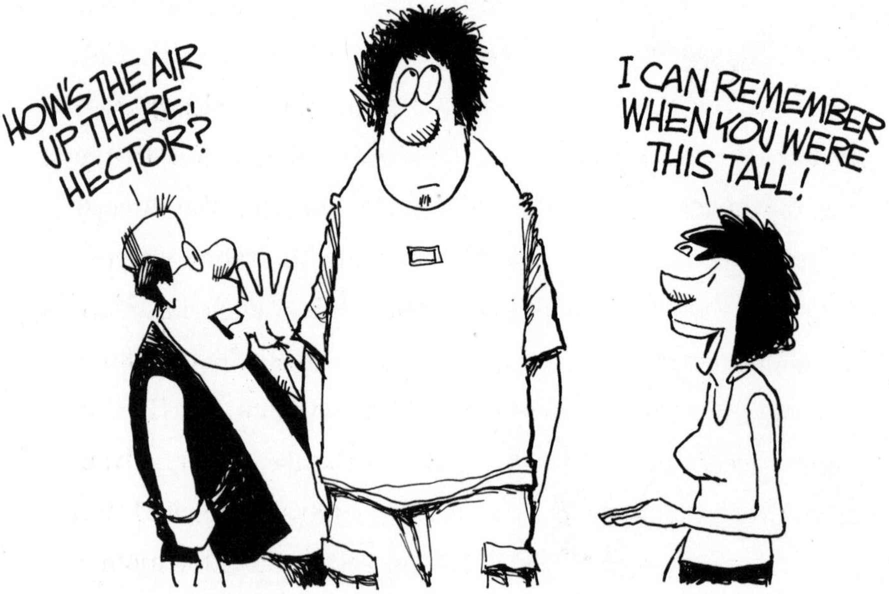
HOW'S THE AIR UP THERE, HECTOR?
I CAN REMEMBER WHEN YOU WERE THIS TALL!

Look, they mean well, but everything would be so much easier if they could just cease to exist on band practice

Saturdays. Is that asking so much? It's not too bad with Hector because he's been around forever and he's got them broken in. But I always cringe when I hear—

DUDES! SOMEBODY TAKE THIS GLOCKENSPIEL BEFORE MY EAR FALLS OFF!

Okay, I'll grant you, my parents are not unique in being confused by our friend Pierce. He's a startling-looking dude at first glance—okay at second and third glance, too. Pierce wears his hair kind of like that smart kid from the Snoopy cartoon—the one with the blanket and the crabby sister— only Pierce's looks like it's been dyed in sangria. He has more metal pinned into and hanging from his head than anybody I know. On a windy day he's a walking wind chime. He also has a ton of tattoos, which he brilliantly uses to his advantage. Every Christmas he goes to the Children's Hospital for a day and lets the sick kids color in his tattoos, and his mom is thrilled. No lame soap baskets or cheesy scarves for his mom. Pierce is a few years older than your average sophomore, having repeated third, fourth, fifth, and seventh grades owing to a few, um, impulse-control issues. You know how some people get an idea and then act on it? Pierce lives the reverse of that. I'm not sure that it's a sustainable lifestyle, but it sure makes school more interesting for everybody. They say that he's single-handedly responsible for tripling the nicotine levels in the faculty lounge. According to his skydiving, bobsledding, X-treme origami, wrist wrestling, nude-yoga-instructor mom, impulse and attention issues sort of run in the family. And when you get to know him, you realize that behind that face of silver beats a heart of gold. Well, not literally behind his face. You know what I mean.

Pierce had just moved to town when our band, Chickenfist, was forming and he asked to audition.

UH, SURE.

His tryout was memorable—just ask anybody in our whole neighborhood. His drum intro set off every car alarm on the block. The extended drum solo caused a permanent change in the migratory patterns of several species of regional birds, and his ginormous cymbal-crashing finale caused minor structural damage to the garage's foundation and loosened the couplings in our yard's sprinkler system. In other words, the audition was a huge success and Pierce became Chickenfist's drummer and designated lunatic on the spot.

Luckily my parents are stunned speechless as Pierce stumbles through the kitchen, and I hustle the guys out to the garage before my mom can offer snickerdoodles, the official cookie of Chickenfist.

We're waiting for Tim, our bass player. It's weird because he's usually on time and he's not answering our texts. So Hector is noodling on some chords to kill time and Pierce is

setting up his thunder sheet, while this random fly harasses us like it's in the band.

It lands on Hector's guitar strings once too often and he starts thrashing at it to chase it away for good. It zips over to my bridge and I slam the whammy bar just as it careens over to Pierce's crash cymbal, and he wails away at it as it flits

across his drum set. Finally it alights contentedly on the amp, shooting us a big toothy grin across its ugly little raisin face. My dad pops his head out the door and says, "Guys, that was awesome! You are *on* it today!"

I'm still trying to finger that "Quintuple Amputee" chord, but it's not sounding right. So I do what any musician does in a situation like this: I blame my equipment.

"I'm thinking ninety percent of the problem is this guitar pick," I say. "Bands like Gingivitis must have some special catalog they order picks from. I mean, how far am I going to get with a flimsy fifty-cent generic pick straight out of the big jar on the counter at Niehaus Music?"

"Dude, these drumsticks were carved from a lotus tree struck by lightning in a sacred Bora-Bora rain forest. They were used by three generations of Nepalese shamans in Himalayan healing ceremonies. I acquired them from a contraband dealer under terms neither of us is free to disclose. I wrap them in my Slayer concert T-shirt and sleep with them under my pillow every night. Get in the game!"

"Okay, hang on," I say. "I think I've got this chord figured out."

With the same wheeling motion I've seen on the Gingivitis video, I take a few practice swings to find my timing and hit the chord. It sounds like a cat passing a kidney stone, and the garage door goes down.

SERIOUSLY?

Where the heck is Tim? Tim was a founding member of the band, too. Hector and I have known him for forever but, now that I think about it, I can't remember how we know him. He's just a random chucklehead who doesn't make a big impression. Tim is one of those guys who seem to have always been around— like French's mustard or the Shins. Guys can be okay with a dude like that.

TIM

It was after the school parking lottery that we really got tight, though. Tim was just a kid who I ran into in the hallway once in a while until the day he pulled a good number in the lottery. See, there are exactly thirty-seven parking spaces for sophomores and juniors who can demonstrate that they carpool with other students. Everybody else has to park in the "Meadow," as the school calls it. The Meadow is actually a nasty, rutted field next to a cow pasture that's full of weeds and discarded pencils, papers, and old calculator batteries. Nobody likes to park out there and I don't understand why the school doesn't just build a parking garage or something. It's almost like they don't want us driving our own cars. Anyway, Tim pulled number thirteen in the lottery and on the way to school the next day, his car accidentally caught fire and sort of blew up. Tim got video of it with his phone, and so far it has 479,000 views on YouTube.

Tim was fine, but that day the three of us formed a strategic alliance. Hector and I would pick Tim up in our van and drive him to school in exchange for the use of his primo parking space. Everybody wins. Well, except Tim, cuz his car is toast.

It was during one of those rides to school that we learned

that he had an old bass guitar and a killer amp that his uncle had given him when he bought a goat cheese farm in Vermont. Tim could play a little (he was into Rob Zombie and Johnny Cash) and he had his own equipment. If forced, he can also sing some harmony. What more was there to know? We had our bass player, and the rest is history. Or, well, it will be someday.

The fly was taunting me now, doing obnoxious little dances on my tuning pegs. I'd study it from the corner of my eye, but when I'd finally make my move, it'd settle contentedly back on the amp.

SNERK!

We're all getting pretty annoyed when finally Tim pulls into the driveway on his moped. He sits there for a while, just kind of star-ing at the handlebars. Then he looks over at my mom, who's pulling weeds in the flower bed, then back at the handlebars. Finally, he rocks the bike back onto the kickstand and slowly unbuckles his helmet.

When he swings his leg off the bike, we can see that there's nothing strapped to the carrier. No guitar. What the—?

"Yeah, dudes, so . . ." he says, shuffling some wires on the garage floor with his feet. The fly crawls into an empty port on the amp and crackles.

". . . count me out today. Maybe for a while."

47

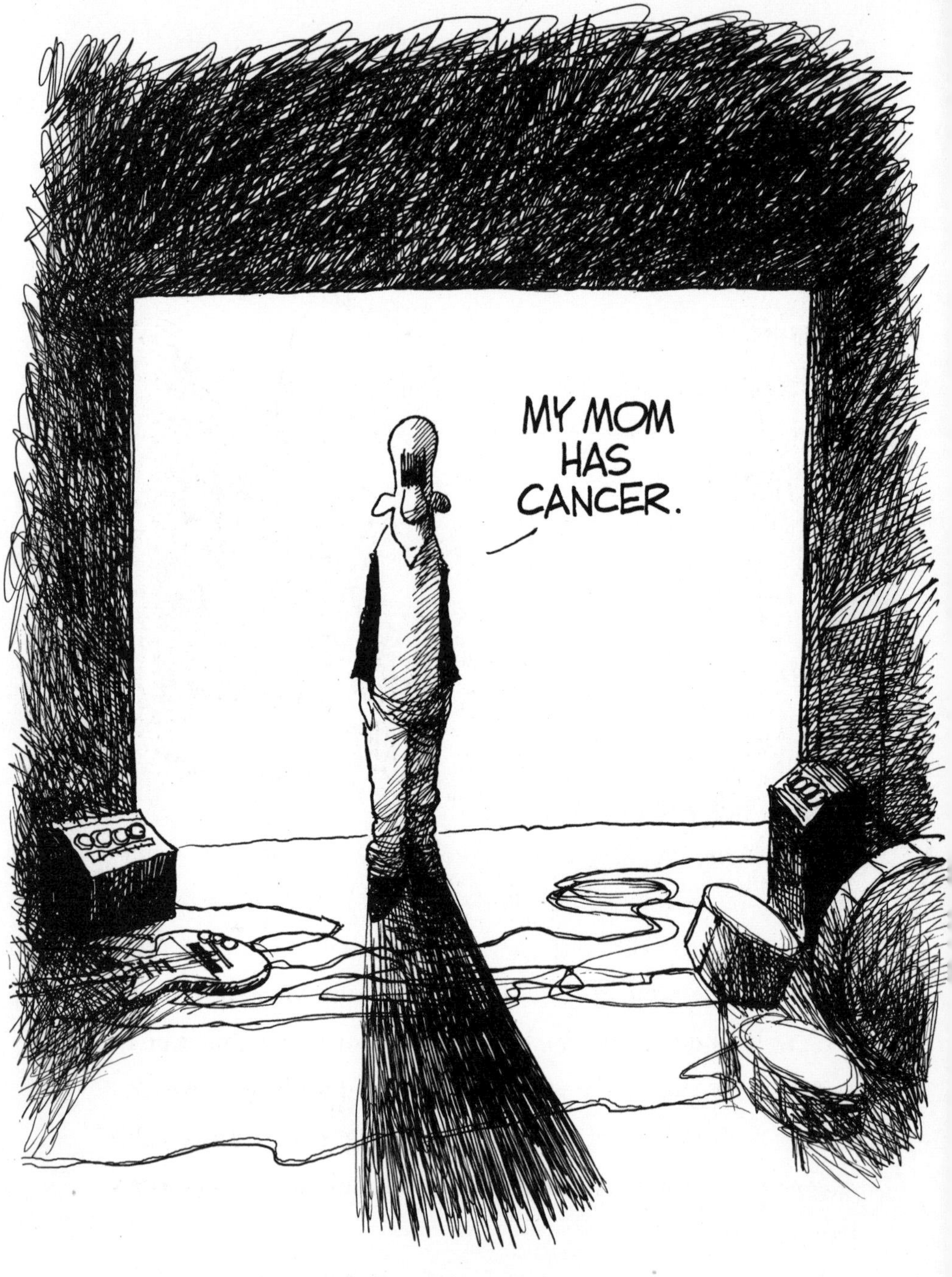
MY MOM HAS CANCER.

CHAPTER 4

You know when you're playing Mutant Meatsucker and you finally defeat the Maggot Overlord, how this kind of heavy silence settles over everything, and nothing moves for forever while you take in the ginormity of it all? Well, it's like that one second after Tim drops the bomb about his mom's cancer thing.

The garage goes completely still except for the sound of

crispy little parts of the electrocuted fly settling to the floor
next to the amp. Finally Hector makes a sound like air escaping
from a tire.

"Pssssssshhhhhhh . . ."

Pierce slumps back and leans his head against an old
license plate hanging on the garage wall. I stare at a spot

on the floor that suddenly starts to intensely bug me. It's
shaped kind of like my middle school gym teacher's head.
Or at least it would be if that big, ugly, flabby flap of skin
that he had on the back of his neck was three times its size
and made out of gum. I snap out of it when Pierce slams his
sticks on his tom-tom and yells:

The sound reverberates around the garage, sending dust and mouse turds raining down from the rafters, adding to the layer of crud already coating the top of the amps.

Everything about this picture is wrong. Saturday band practice is supposed to be an escape from whatever crap you've put up with that week, not new crap that the universe has invented when you weren't looking! Tim is supposed to be this guy you don't have to think about. Plus, Tim's mom is one of our biggest supporters and happens to be the hottest mom we know, making this doubly unfair. This is not a subject I want to dwell on, but it's worth mentioning again because it's so true. She's really decent looking, has a great smile, and she doesn't have that momish smell (which, after some study, I have identified as a cross between Swiss cheese and hand lotion). The woman is unique among other elderly women in their early forties. Comparing Tim's mom to the average mom would be like comparing a double-decker bacon cheeseburger to a cow. I mean, on some level they're basically the same thing, but one is a beautiful and evolved creation of nature, and the other one is a cow.

I look at the stupid gym teacher gum spot on the floor again, and my mind flashes back to the freshman winter formal. It was Chickenfist's first official gig and T-Mom volunteered to be our roadie and driver since none of us had a license at the time. Her name is Sandy, but to us she's Tim's mom, or T-Mom. My mom is J-Mom, Pierce's mom is P-Mom, and Hector's mom is Rosalita because Rosalita is such an awesome name. I can't remember which one of us came up with that whole system, but it works.

AND IT TURNS OUT THESE ARE VEGAN!

Twizzler

"I really can't lift that much," T-Mom said. "And the van smells like French fries, but the rear seat comes out and I think all of your stuff will fit back there. There are bungee cords in case you need to strap some of the drums to the roof, and there's a box of Slim Jims back there because you'll need some protein if you're going to keep them dancing all night."

That was so cool of her.

My mom's idea was to have each of our parents drive us separately to the dance. How creative. But that's her. I mean, my mom is practical and everything, but not what

WOW, YOUR FIRST JIG!

IF ONLY GRANDMA COULD SEE YOU NOW!

DID YOU BRUSH YOUR TEETH?

YOU SHOULD PLAY 'PROUD MARY.'

LAME

you would call edgy. Or progressive. I mean, every room in our house but mine is painted Latte, Oatmeal, Mushroom, or Biscuit. The average person could die from beige poisoning by just walking through the place.

T-Mom, on the other hand, understood the Zeitgeist of the Gig.

Somehow she instinctively knew that the band

OPPOSITE OF LAME

DUDE

needed to travel together, knew to stay out of the way and knew not to get all chatty in the process. When a group of guys is about to get up onstage in front of a gym full of sweaty teenagers and wary chaperones, the last thing they want to hear from their roadie is "How's school?" or "Does anybody have to go to the bathroom?"

At some point, I guess my mom must have drifted over from weeding the flower bed to overhearing us in the garage, because I look up and see her arm slip gently around Tim's shoulder. He doesn't flinch. "How are you feeling, Tim?" she says.

"Well, I'm just—" he starts.

"Mom, please!" I say. "Can't you just give a guy a chance not to talk about it?"

I will never understand most females. They think you have to beat everything to death with words. They take the simplest little thought, strap it to a chair, and throttle it senseless with a month's worth of words. What's the point? Guys operate way more economically. We can say a lot with a few well-placed *dude*s.

But girls act like there's a prize for squeezing the most words into a room.

Tim slips away from my mom's sympathy death grip and shuffles back toward the door.

"Anyway. I can't practice today because I've got to go to the doctor with my mom," Tim says. Then he squats down and starts to untwist a couple of cables on the floor that don't really need untwisting. "I took some tests and it turns out I'm a match as a bone marrow donor for her. The night of the Gingivitis concert I'll be in the hospital getting the bone marrow sucked out of my hip for her procedure."

"Oh, Tim," my mom says, "you're going through an awful lot."

"It is what it is," he says. But he sounds a little phlegmy and the gum spot on the floor suddenly gets really interesting again. And then I realize something.

"Dude, that's why you sold us your tickets," I text. "We just thought you were a chucklehead."

Tim reads my text, smiles a little, and shrugs as he stands up and heads over to his moped. He slips on his helmet, buckles it, then texts me back,

"Yeah, well, there'll be other once-in-a-lifetime opportunities."

Tim's moped sputters down the street like my grandpa on burrito night, and the rest of us just stand there, staring at one another. Ordinarily it cracks me up whenever that farty little engine of his revs up, but this time it's just a lonely drone that echoes off houses, mailboxes, and elm trees until it's absorbed into the Saturday sounds of lawn mowers, leaf blowers, and parents ragging on their kids.

"Dude," Pierce sighs.

"Dude," goes Hector.

"Dude," I agree. And that pretty much says it all.

After a while Pierce starts laying down a beat and we all try to muscle through the first verse of the old Garbage Truck standard "It's All Over but the Leeching," but it isn't happening.

We barely sound okay with a bass player. Without one, the suckage factor is off the charts. Besides, it's hard to focus on anything upbeat, so we decide to pack it in. As Hector and I are lugging the gong toward Pierce's car, Sara and D'ijon pull up. After what we just went through, seeing their faces is like pizza after an SAT test.

"NOOOO! We missed EVERYTHING?" says Sara. "We just stopped for five seconds to bring you some caramel macarenas and practice is already over?" she says, handing grandes all around. Macarenas. Macchiatos. I give her a big hug, partly because I need one and partly because she mangles the English language in such adorable ways.

"Yuh. Tim sort of dropped a bomb on us," I say, looking at the guys. "His mom has cancer. He's going to be her bone marrow donor."

"Ohmygawd," says D'ijon, covering her mouth with both hands and falling back against the car.

"Is he all right?" asks Sara.

"All right how?" I ask.

"All right like all right! All right like coping with the shock. All right like helping his dad deal with everything. All right like even wrapping his mind around the crapiosity of the situation. All right like handling the

OH MY GA WD!

fact that he's basically saving his mom's life. All right like dealing with the whole emotional cluster bomb that JUST WENT OFF IN HIS LIFE!!"

"Um, he didn't say."

"He didn't say?" she says. "HE DIDN'T SAY!?"

"I'm pretty sure he's fine," I add.

It goes back to the basic difference between girls and guys, I think. When girls deal with each other it's like three-dimensional chess. Guys keep things simpler.

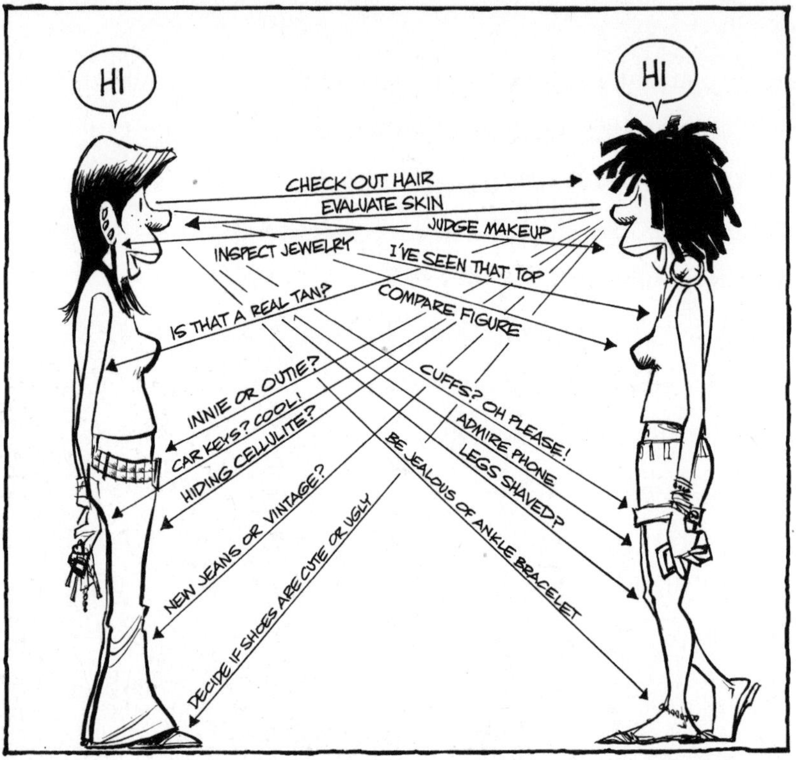
HI
HI
CHECK OUT HAIR
EVALUATE SKIN
JUDGE MAKEUP
INSPECT JEWELRY
I'VE SEEN THAT TOP
IS THAT A REAL TAN?
COMPARE FIGURE
INNIE OR OUTIE?
CAR KEYS? COOL!
HIDING CELLULITE?
CUFFS? OH PLEASE!
ADMIRE PHONE
LEGS SHAVED?
BE JEALOUS OF ANKLE BRACELET
NEW JEANS OR VINTAGE?
DECIDE IF SHOES ARE CUTE OR UGLY

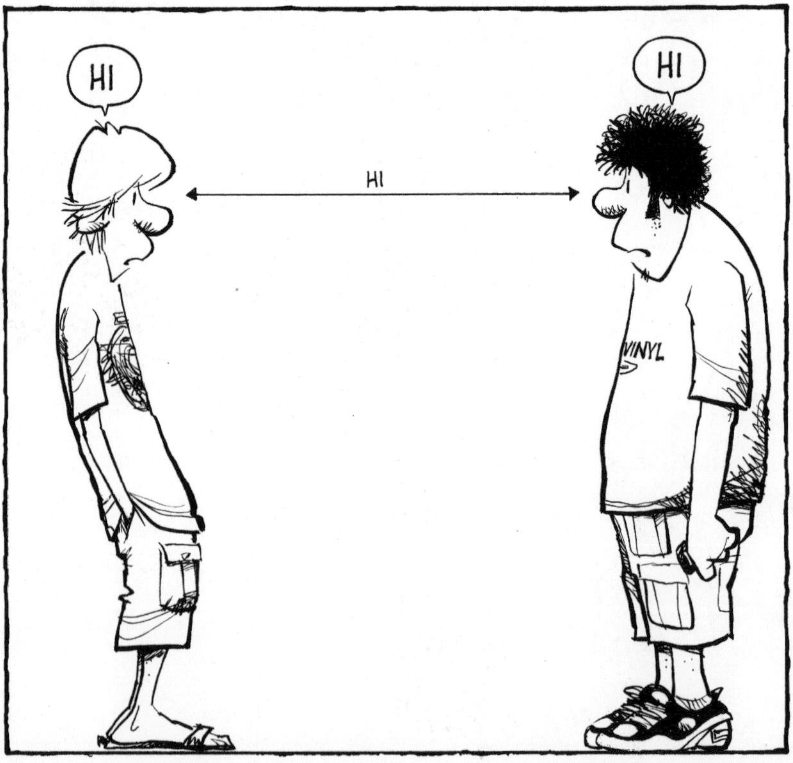
HI
HI
HI
VINYL

Sara gives me a flat, cold stare and says:

DID YOU HAPPEN TO **ASK** HIM, JEREMY?

and I get the same sinking feeling in my gut that I get during Mutant Meatsucker when the game turns me into a T-bone steak and the Maggot Overlord towers above me.

HONESTLY!

"Not in so many words," I croak.

Bee-yooup! I'm devoured. Game over.

* * *

After dinner I'm helping my dad clean up by watching him scrape the barbecue grill. I told you that he's an orthodontist, so I suppose it's no surprise that he can't stand the sight of a dirty grill. He attacks the barbecue like it's a patient with a mouthful of

Oreos. I am not kidding. He actually flosses the grate. Out of boredom I finally mumble, "Sara's mad at me."

"Mad at you? What for?" he asks.

"I dunno. Something about Tim, I think. Or something I said. Or didn't say. It's pretty hard to tell because she was wearing that light blue tank top that always distracts me. All I know is that I need to think of a way to fix it."

I can see my dad slipping into TED talk mode, where he suddenly turns into a World Expert on some stupid subject

that we happen to be talking about at the time. It looks like I'm going to be here for a while. He picks up a spatula and motions for me to sit in the lawn chair next to his. I slide my phone out of my pocket to a discreet spot behind my leg so I can play Words With Friends while I listen deeply to his pearls of wisdom.

"Let me tell you something about relationships, Jeremy," he begins, shaking his greasy spatula at me for emphasis. "Guys think the key to a good relationship is saying the right thing, solving problems," he says. "We think that when someone has a complaint or gets mad at us, we should be able to come up with an answer that solves it or makes it go away. That's what we do—we solve problems, right? But that's all wrong, Jeremy. The key to relationships is listening."

A O I U L I A. Great. All I can spell are Hawaiian words.

"Uh-huh," I say.

"Women and girls thrive on connection. It's what drives them. You'll find that if you open up and share what's really inside you, all the other little spats and quarrels will evaporate."

"Mmm," I say.

Is *aluai* a word? Isn't that a bird?

"Here's the secret: The next time you're with Sara, ask her how she's feeling and—here's the important part—really listen to her answer."

"And?"

"That's it. Really listen. See what happens."

"Thanks, Dad," I say, getting up. "You are a fountain of aioli. And I'd love to talk all night, but I have to go!"

I make my break, and as I'm hurdling the hedge, he aims another thought at me.

"Bonus tip," he hollers, pausing for dramatic effect. "It works for guy friends, too."

"ThanksI'llkeepitinmind," I say and I dive into the van before he can slam another wisdom clip into his emotional AK-47. I'm supposed to pick up Hector and Pierce and Sara and D'ijon because everybody is hanging out tonight back here at my house—

—if I can get the van to start.

CHAPTER 5

If you have ever dropped a cell phone into a running garbage disposal while you are trying to wipe off a skillet (not my fault, but my dad still harasses me about texting while drying), then you know what the van's engine sounds like when it starts up. Cell phone in a disposal, gravel in a blender . . . it's hard to come up with an exact description of the sound, but let's just say that it's not good.

The noise probably has something to do with the van's starter motor, but the thing still kind of works, so we haven't fixed it. Or had it fixed. Or asked our dads to lend us the money to have it fixed. Hector and I figure that if something almost, usually, or even occasionally works, that's good enough for us. Besides, it's no surprise that a van that's on its third odometer would have some issues, right? As future rock gods, we have a duty to live insane risk-taking and unstructured lives.

Naturally, being sixteen years old and living at home limits those options a little, so a wonky starter motor is the best we can do in that depart- ment for now.

So I'm sitting in the van, ready to leave. I take a deep, cleansing breath and stare deep into the unblinking eye of the speedometer. . . .

"Hi Van. It's me, Jeremy." I'm usually not this formal with machines, but old and cranky things seem to work better when they feel respected. It's knowledge I've acquired from years of living with my parents. "I need to pick up Hector, Sara, Pierce, and D'ijon, so I'm going to ask you to give me a hand with that, okay?"

My relationship with the van is complicated. I'm just half owner, but where Hector sees a machine, I see a struggling spirit. Our van has a soul and a personality and, yeah, kind of a poor attitude at times, but this is the Holy Grail of classic Volkswagen vans and must be treated with respect and dignity. One does not just turn the key in a 1962 VW Split-Window Kombi and expect it to start right up. Trust me, Stephen Hawking couldn't figure out the exact combination of factors involved on his first try.

The passenger door only must be locked.

The driver's window must be open 3 inches and facing NNW at 333°

The radio must be tuned to ZROCK 103.7.

The humidity level must be below 60% with winds from the SW.

The constellation Andromeda must be visible between latitudes 90 and -40 degrees.

It took Hector and me months of trial, error, more error, and plenty of words that our moms would consider inappropriate to figure out how to get the thing to start. It was sort of an accident that we came upon the ignition-by-retainer method that we use now.

One Saturday we had the engine cover up while we were trying to see why the van smelled skunky.

"Try tapping on something with the screwdriver," Hector suggested.

"Brilliant idea, amigo," I said, as I reached for the screwdriver in my back pocket. Maybe it wasn't a brilliant idea, but it was better than nothing, which is what I was doing. "What part of an engine smells like skunk, anyway?"

The answer to that question was (and still is) every part if, as in our case, an actual skunk happened to be sleeping in your engine compartment. As I was tapping around, I

accidentally touched these two metal parts with the screwdriver at the same time. The key must have been in the On position because all at once, there was an electrical crackling sound, a bright flash, and the engine just started on its own.

And FYI, Flaming Rocket Skunk could be the next big thing in the world of fireworks. Hector and I spent the rest of the day soaking in tomato juice and trying to replicate the event (minus the skunk part). I still think there was some kind of divine intervention or genius on my part that helped us discover that Hector's retainer was the perfect tool for this operation. He says it's because he sneezed and the thing flew out of his mouth and started the engine again. Whatever.

But since Hector and his retainer aren't here right now, I have to start the engine the old way. I mentally run through the checklist one more time, give the steering wheel a little kiss, and gently but firmly turn the key. I hear a familiar rattle

of parts and the van farts a cloud of chunky black smoke before chugging to life. We have ignition! I breathe a sigh of relief and thank the gods of German engineering that I don't have to ask to borrow my dad's Civic.

As I'm fastening my seat belt my mind flashes back to the first time Hector and I saw the van. It was sitting behind the barn belonging to this old hippie farmer. We had talked our dads into driving us way out past Bucyrus to check it out, and it was even more beautiful than the two-inch-square black-and-white picture in the *Auto Swapper* ad showed.

The paint had aged to a suedelike finish the color of the freckles on Sara's shoulders. The chipped flower power decals randomly covering the sides and the roof were faded, and somebody had once spray-painted a peace sign on the door. The rear had once been covered in bumper stickers, you could tell, and we could still make out a few. Even the cement blocks it sat on looked retro and cool.

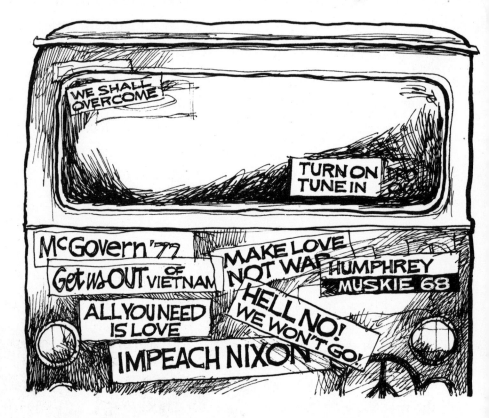

"She's a beauty, isn't she," the farmer said. It wasn't really a question. He knew it, and Hector and I knew it; this was our baby.

"I picked up Janis Joplin hitchhiking to Woodstock in this van," the farmer said as he wiped a little tear from his eye. "Followed the Grateful Dead for five years in it, and

took it to Burning Man a couple of times back when they still held it on Baker Beach. Believe it or not, Arlo Guthrie wrote the first two verses of 'Alice's Restaurant' while sobering up in the rear seat."

If we had not been students of ancient rock history this may have sounded like gibberish, but Hector and I have spent a billion hours studying the liner notes on the album covers my dad has stashed in the basement. We may be the only people under fifty who have ever heard of the Blues Magoos or Iron Butterfly. So some of what the farmer was saying actually gave me chills.

We stuck our heads inside the van, and the smell of fifty-year-old patchouli and wet wool filled our noses. We looked up and noticed that the headliner was missing, along with a chunk of the roof about the size of a large pizza box.

"On a clear night, you can lean back and watch the constellations from the driver's seat." The farmer sighed.

S-o-o-o-o cool.

I tried to remember what my dad had told me about negotiation: Play it slowly, don't act too interested right away, and whatever you do, let the seller make the first move. So I made the first move.

"I can't remember . . . how much were you asking for it?"

The farmer snerked up a loogie, spit, and smiled. "Well, that ad you have there in your hand says three hundred bucks."

"Three hundred, huh?" I nodded and spit, too. "Let me talk to my amigo." Hector and I huddled off to the side.

"Why did you spit on my shoe?" Hector hissed.

"Strategy. So what do you think? Should we buy it?"

"It needs some work."

"True. I heard our dads talking, and they think that restoring a vehicle could be a valuable learning experience for us. They think it could teach us responsibility, goal setting, and follow-through."

Hector thought for a second, then said, "Well, I think we should do it, anyway."

"Agreed." About that time, our dads walked over. "Now what?" I asked. Hector's dad put his hands in his pockets and took a step back.

My dad shrugged. "This is your deal, boys. You talk to the guy," he said. My dad looked over his shoulder at the farmer, then back at Hector and me and whispered, "But don't pay the asking price . . . negotiate with him." And they moved off. Hector and I put our heads together again, did some quick math, and made a decision.

"We'll give you two hundred ninety-five."

"Deal," said the farmer.

The oil smoke surrounding the van is starting to lift, so I group text everybody, throw my phone in my backpack, and ease the van onto the mean streets of Yellow Duckling Creek.

About an hour later Sara, Pierce, D'ijon, Hector, and I are hanging out when we hear, "Who wants to play Cranium?" It's one of my mom's ways of letting us know she's heading down to see what we're doing. I think she imagines that every time she turns her back we're playing naked Twister or something. She's also been known to have these unstoppable late-night urges to fold laundry, get luggage from the storage room, or

dust the top of the backup refrigerator in the basement when I have my friends over . . . especially when some of them are girls. She thinks we don't realize why she's barging in, but it's pretty obvious.

The truth is that nothing happens when my friends get together in my basement rec room. At least nothing that my mom would understand. It's way too chill to be intercepted by parental radar. We just hang out and say or do stupid stuff until somebody spews Sprite out his nose and then we make fun of one another until everybody has to go home.

WOULDN'T IT BE FUN TO PUT ON A TALENT SHOW?

The surest way I know to make my friends laugh is when I do this patented dance I've perfected. I invented it one night when Hector had had like six Dr Peppers and he started making up this song about cheese-flavored underwear. (I know, stupid, right?) Pierce started beating on his djembe with this reggae rhythm, and I jumped up and just started spazz dancing.

At first I was just gooning around, but then I started getting into it. It was maybe the first time in my life that dancing felt like anything but torture. It was awesome, like my body was

suddenly taken over by wild happy demons. Everything was fluid, pulsing with the rhythm of the drum, and they say that I had this stupid grin on my face that wouldn't go away.

Everybody jumped up and a new dance experience was born. You watch—someday it will go viral.

YOU LOOK LIKE YOU'RE MILKING A KANGAROO!

This isn't that kind of a night, though. We keep trying to spark some goofiness, but it's like the fuse is wet. I guess Tim and his mom are on everybody's minds. At least I know they're on mine.

"I keep thinking we should do something for Tim and his mom," Sara says. "I mean, come on! Tim is our friend and his mom needs his bone mallow and he needs our support! I would so run a 5K right now for him."

"Bone marrow. And I'd do that 5K if I could get those cute Reeboks we saw the other day," says D'ijon.

"Ohmygawd! You mean those lime green ones with the yellow soles? Those were soooo cute," squeals Sara. "They would be perfect with my black running shorts! Do you want to borrow them?"

"Borrow them? I loaned them to *you*, girl," D'ijon shoots back.

"Could everybody just shut up for a second," I yell. "There is no 5K! There's only Tim and his mom and this huge, crappy situation, which nobody is doing anything about! Come on! We should all stop thinking about ourselves and start thinking about how we're going to be there for Tim!" The room goes silent. "I mean, except for Hector and me, who will be at the Gingivitis concert that night having the best time of our lives," I kind of mumble. More silence. The uncomfortable kind.

"Which is why"—I'm rallying—"which is why Hector and I will not be going to the concert to have the best time of our lives!"

"What!?" yelps Hector.

"We will be going to the Gingivitis concert to have the best time of our lives for Tim," I say, not really even believing it myself.

*For Tim

"I mean, once we get permission from our parents and everything." More silence.

Then D'ijon jumps up and starts flapping her hands.

"You guys! Maybe we should do that thing where we all shave our heads so Tim's mom won't feel so alone when her hair falls out!" Whenever D'ijon gets excited she does this hand-flapping thing that makes her look like her fingers are on fire or something. Then she stops, cocks a hip, makes a big circle in the air with her right index finger, and points to her dreads.

"And I say that as a person with trademark-able hair."

We all look around the room, trying to imagine one another bald.

"I've heard of people doing that," Sara finally says, "but I have a hair appointment on Thursday. What if I just got my split ends cut off instead of shaving my whole head? That would still be kind of supportive, right?"

Then everybody starts arguing about what we should do to help Tim. Everybody except Pierce, who just disappears up the stairs toward the bathroom.

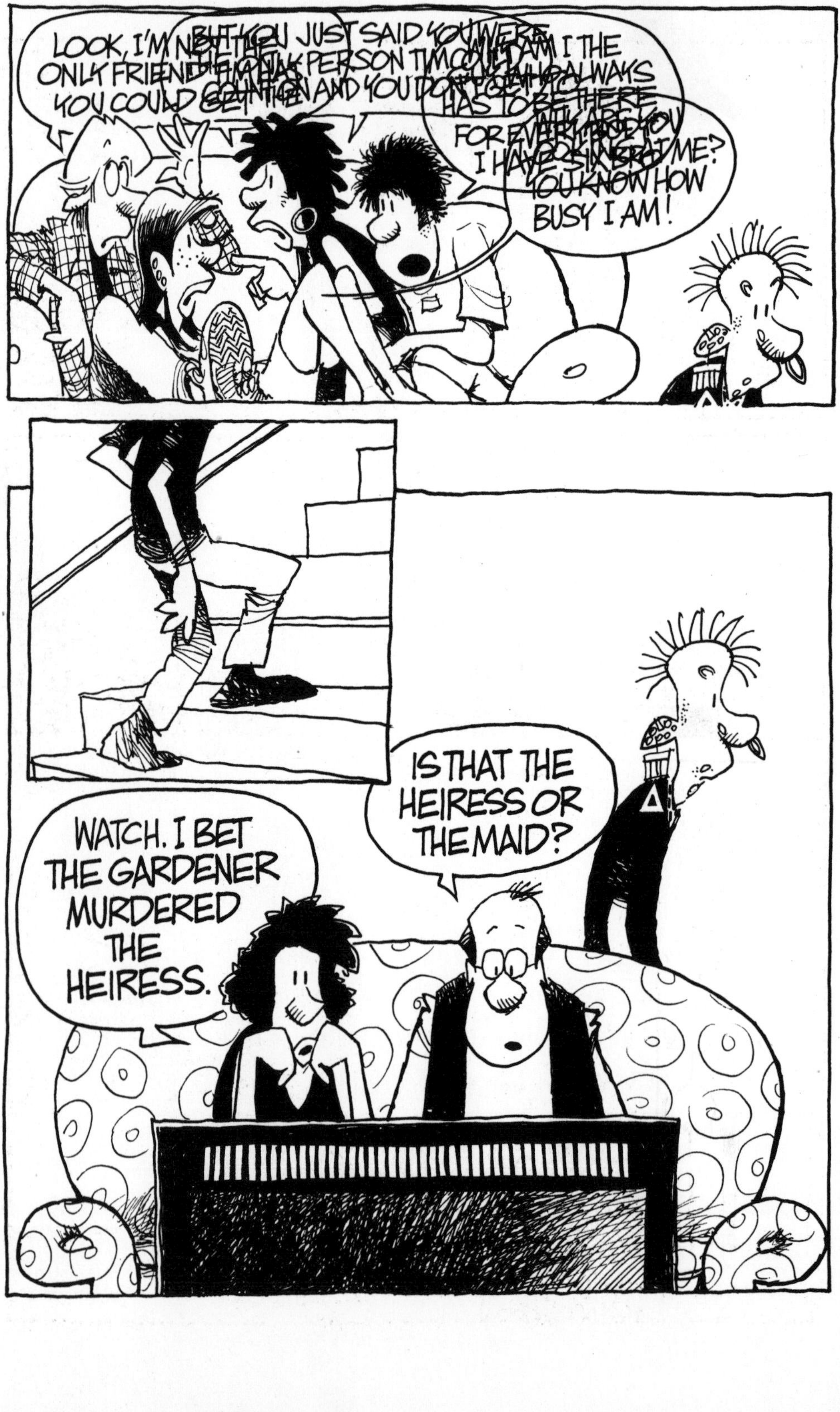
YOU KNOW HOW BUSY I AM!
WATCH. I BET THE GARDENER MURDERED THE HEIRESS.
IS THAT THE HEIRESS OR THE MAID?

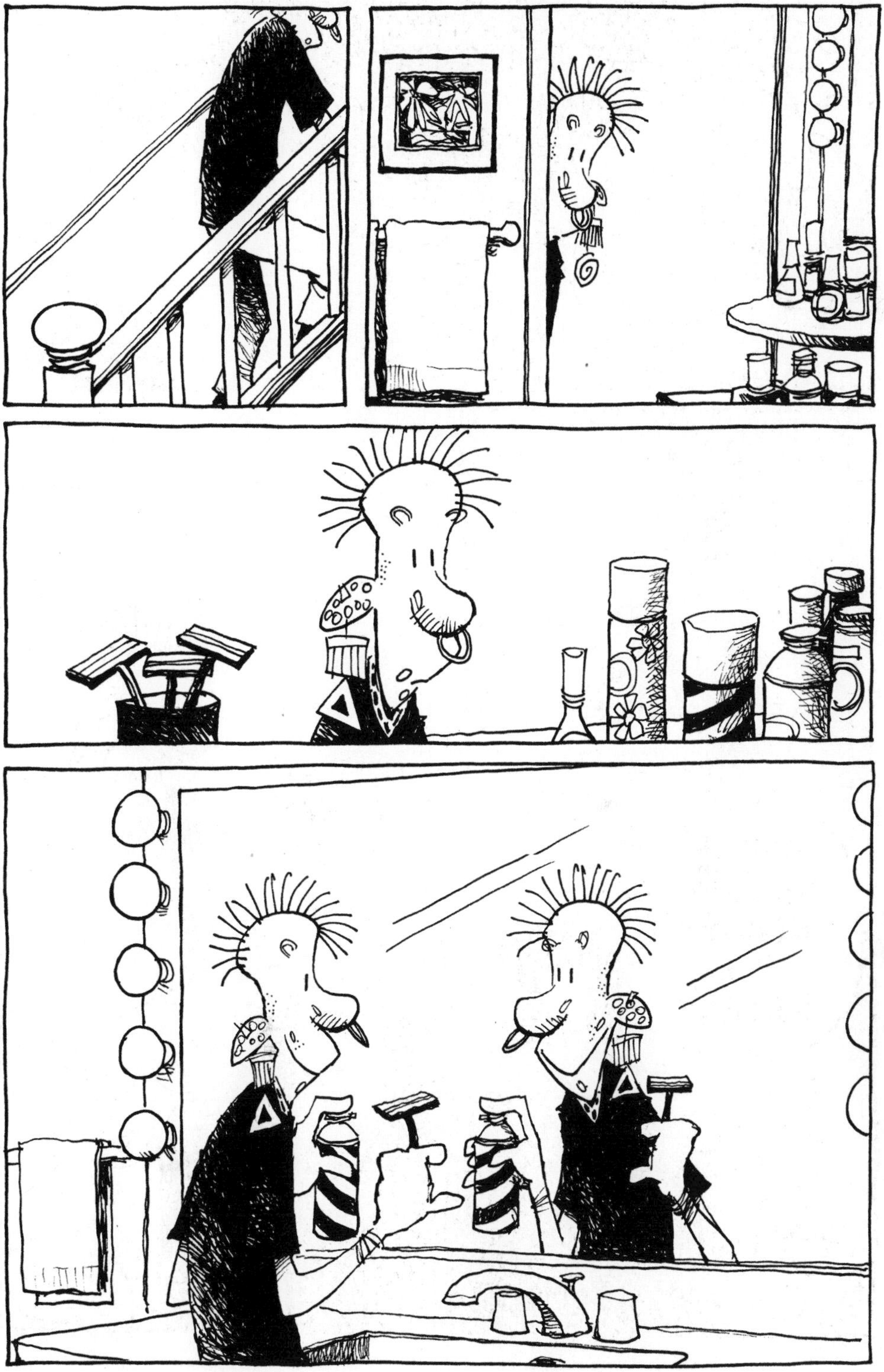

"All I'm saying is that shaving your head isn't the ONLY way to show your support," Hector yells.

"That's right! And all I'm saying is that supporting your fellow human beans should involve more than a bad haircut five weeks before prom," adds Sara.

The conversation in the rec room is getting pretty heated and is all about who cares more and who's going to be more supportive of Tim during the bone marrow harvest (*eww*) procedure. It's pretty much coming down to Sara and D'ijon spending the night at the hospital with Tim while Hector and I go to the Gingivitis concert in solidarity with our fallen brother. I keep trying to make that okay in my head, but it's not working. This situation calls for some kind of selfless act, like the time my mom had the flu for seven days and I put my own ice cream bowl in the dishwasher without being told to. Then Pierce walks back down the stairs.

Everybody stops and stares at his head, which is not just hairless as an ice rink, but looks like the Zamboni has been across it once or twice, too.

Hector and I exchange guilty looks as I run my hand through my hair and swallow hard. Hector shrugs like it's no big deal, which it probably isn't for a guy who can grow sideburns and a Fu Manchu during lunch hour. My hair grows at the speed of an afternoon algebra class. Everyone is looking at me.

Time to man up.

CHAPTER 6

"Pierce . . . dude . . ." We're all sitting there staring at this gleaming bald head of his. I'm trying to think of what else to say when Sara snickers, then Hector snorts a mouthful of Mountain Dew into his elbow, and pretty soon we're all cracking up.

D'ijon starts rubbing Pierce's head like it was some kind

of crystal ball, which it sort of literally is. I can see my future there, and it is not what I had in mind. It's taken almost three months for my hair to grow back after the tragic haircut my mom forced on me before we took this year's Christmas card picture.

Seriously. Imagine that it's the middle of August, and on a perfectly good Saturday your mom makes you haul an artificial Christmas tree out of the attic and set it up in the living room. Yeah, that's right, and it gets worse. Then you have to climb back into the attic (where it's about a billion degrees, by the way) and find all the decorations. Then, in full view of the neighborhood, you and your parents decorate the fake

Christmas tree, put on epically ugly, matching sweaters, and take pictures of yourselves with your dad's new digital camera. That's my mom for you. Always planning ahead in order to keep us running at full dorkage.

I rub my hand over my hair, maybe just to feel it for the last time. Then Sara screams, "Ohmygawd, Pierce! Your head is so shiny! I'm putting this on my Facebook right now!" She is one with the phone. The girl has Olympic-class thumb speed. I've never seen anyone who's as fast as she is . . . or as inaccurate. She's not a bad speller; she just gives autocorrect more authority than it deserves and never looks back. You know how she mangles words sometimes? It's the same thing when she texts, only funnier because it's in writing. I saved this exchange we had the other day:

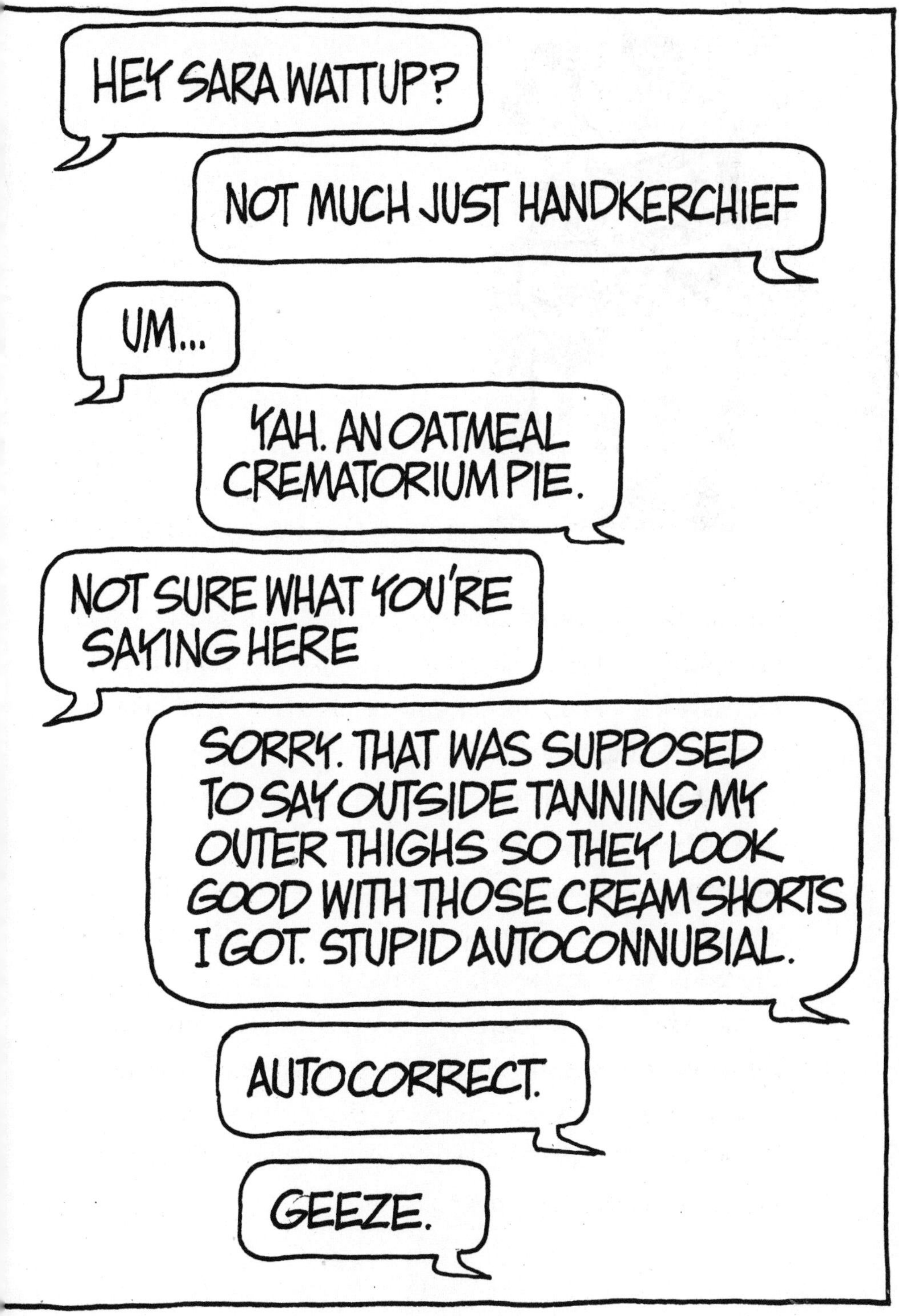
HEY SARA WATTUP?
NOT MUCH JUST HANDKERCHIEF
UM...
YAH. AN OATMEAL CREMATORIUM PIE.
NOT SURE WHAT YOU'RE SAYING HERE
SORRY. THAT WAS SUPPOSED TO SAY OUTSIDE TANNING MY OUTER THIGHS SO THEY LOOK GOOD WITH THOSE CREAM SHORTS I GOT. STUPID AUTOCONNUBIAL.
AUTOCORRECT.
GEEZE.

Pierce points to his phone. "Don't bother posting. It's already on my Facebook and on the screens of all three thousand of my friends."

Pierce is grinning while he says this, which makes him look like a skinny Buddha.

D'ijon looks like she's going to pee her pants.

"He . . . looks . . . so . . . adorable!" D'ijon can hardly get a sentence out between gasps. I have to admit, once you get over the initial shock, Pierce really does rock the shaved-head look. I'm starting to feel a little better about this. I mean, how bad could it be, really? It's only hair, and it might be kind of cool to see what my head looks like shaved.

NAKED MOLE RAT

OR NOT.

There's a creak on the steps and we hear,

Everybody turns around and my parents are standing there looking at Pierce and trying to form words. Pierce, being Pierce and everything, is used to dumbfounded adults and it doesn't bother him at all. He puts his arm around my mom's shoulder and says, "Hey, Mrs. D. Thanks for letting me use your bathroom. That shaving cream you use on your legs is amazing! My head has never felt so sexy smooth. Oh, and you might want to toss that razor."

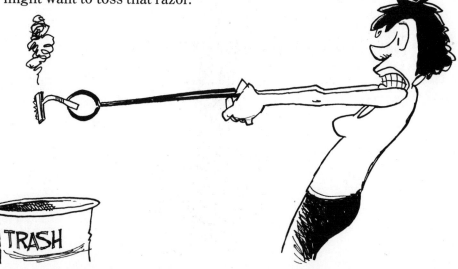

My mom starts to say something, but stops and slowly shakes her head. A phone vibrates and everybody moves to see if it's theirs, like some kind of synchronized telecommunication ballet.

Sara texts something—I swear, her thumbs move like a meerkat after a double espresso—then jumps up and kisses me on the cheek. She grabs D'ijon and drags her past my parents, who are still staring at Pierce with their mouths hanging open.

"Gotta go. Thanks, Mr. D.! Thanks, Mrs. D.!"

D'ijon pauses for a second and waves her hand in front of my mom's eyes. No reaction. She looks at me with her "What th—" face and then smiles. Sara's mom honks the horn in the driveway, then Sara giggles, waves, and they run up the stairs, hanging on to each other and laughing hysterically.

My dad says, "Wh—," then sort of shakes his head and leaves, too.

"Pierce, what made you decide to shave your head, sweetie?" Uh-oh. My mom has shifted into psychotherapist mode. I'd recognize it anywhere. Her eyes sort of go half closed, she tents her fingers, and lowers the screech factor in her voice about seven clicks. She does this all the time, and it drives me nuts. As if it's not bad enough to have a mom who's always trying to find out what you're doing, I have to have one who also wants to know why.

"Why are you feeling this way? Why are you choosing to do that? Why do you think this is happening to you?" It's annoying. Sometimes there is no why. There is just because. Or why not. Or sometimes I dunno. Life is complicated only if you want it to be. That's the way I look at it, at least.

Anyway when my mom asks Pierce what made him decide to shave his head, he gives her an honest answer:

"'Duderonomy'?" she repeats, psychotherapist-style.

"Right. It's the practice of being a true dude by treating a fellow dude with respect and compassion."

"Um-hmm . . ." It's pretty obvious to me that my mom has absolutely no idea what Pierce is talking about. It's subtle, but basically, when she acts like she knows what you're talking about, it means that she's clueless.

The basement windows are open, so I can hear the sound of a muffler dragging up our driveway. It stops, then there's a soft, muffled buzzing sound. After a couple of minutes of that there's a clattering coming from the kitchen upstairs that sounds like some-body's hooked a dozen tambourines to a Jack Russell terrier.

Pierce's mom has arrived. P-Mom is this weird, funny, technically crazy lady who's always pushing her latest obses-sion on everybody she sees. And she has a

NAMASTE, Y'ALL!

lot of obsessions. Last month it was political reflexology, and Pierce says she gave free foot rubs to the whole city council during a meeting. Next month it might be gerbil farming or cross-country roller skating. You never know, but it's always fun to watch people react to her. She looks back at my dad and hands him a jelly jar full of some kind of green mucus. He points at the jar.

"Kale, beet tops, jabuticaba, and okra," she explains. "It's totally healthy, and once you get past the taste and the texture, you're going to love it. Juicing is life, Walt!"

My mom stands up and walks over to P-Mom, looking all

apologetic. She gestures at Pierce and says, "Tawny, I—"

"It's not Tawny anymore," P-Mom interrupts. "I'm calling myself Burkina Faso to highlight the struggle of the endangered West African mountain mud turtles."

Blink. Blink. My mom stares at P-Mom for a second, processing this information while making a quick stability analysis on her. "Right," my mom says. "Anyway, I was going to say that we didn't know Pierce was going to shave his head, but apparently he did it out of compassion for Tim and his mom, so we hope you . . ."

Dude. This is awesome. I haven't seen my parents so stupefied since they found out I'd been washing my athletic cup in the dishwasher (we ate off paper plates for, like, a week). P-Mom is way proud of herself and throws a meaty arm around Pierce's neck.

"I checked Pierce's Facebook page in the driveway a few minutes ago. I thought shaving his head was such a beautiful act of compassion for T-Mom that I had to support him by doing it, too." Pierce and his mom touch bald heads in kind of a nogginized high five.

"You carry a shaver in your car?" asks my dad.

"Absolutely. If you'd sutured as many injured opossums as I have, you'd carry one, too. By the way, you're welcome to use it to finish the job on your head. You missed a couple of sprigs of hair on the sides." My dad starts to say something, but then he just adjusts his comb-over and flops down into a beanbag chair. Tactical error. It takes my dad, like, an hour to get out of a beanbag. Maybe he's forgotten about that, or maybe he's settling in for a long family discussion. Either way, he's not going anywhere until my mom releases him by helping him up. P-Mom/ Burkina Faso looks at her watch and pats Pierce on the shoulder. "Piercey, we have to go."

Pierce pulls the hat his mom was wearing onto his own head and they both laugh. Then they head upstairs, looking a little like Larry and Curly from the Three Stooges from behind. I snap a quick photo for weirdness and a possible future home screen for my phone.

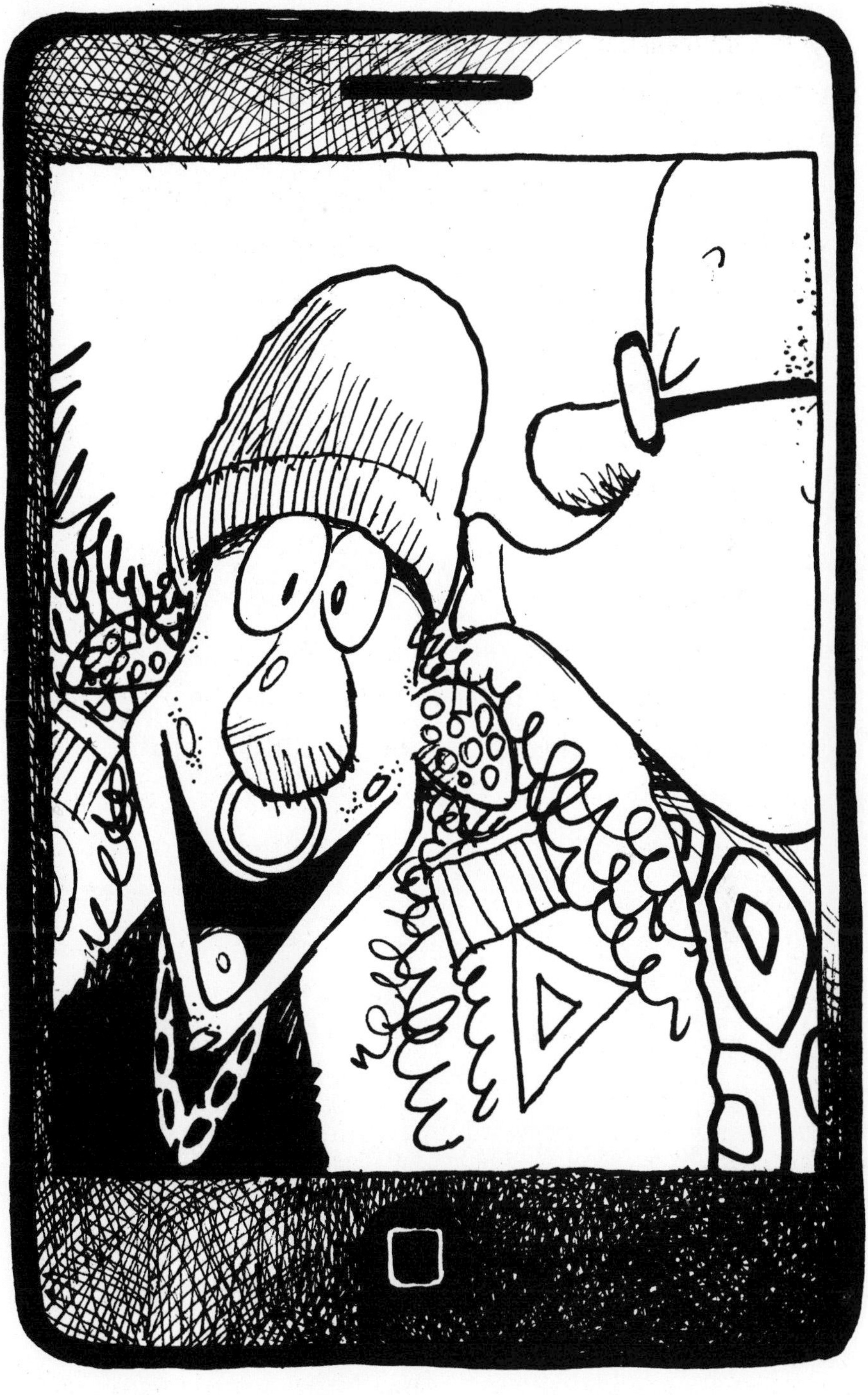

Hector and I sit on the couch and my mom plops down in the beanbag next to my dad. She sighs and then says, "Talk to us."

I shrug. "I dunno. This has been a pretty crazy day. It's bad enough that Tim's mom has cancer, but we found out that Sara and D'ijon are sacrificing their entire Saturday night to be with Tim at the hospital during the bone marrow procedure."

"That's really sweet of them," my dad says.

"Yeah, well, then Pierce and his weird mom—"

"Don't call Tawny names—or what was it? Burkina Faso? Anyway, don't call her weird. She's um, passionate, that's all," my dad says, accidentally taking a sip of the green muck in his hand. He winces, swallows, and then sets the jar down as far away from himself as he can without actually having to get out of the beanbag to do it.

"Okay, Pierce and his passionate mom—if you don't think that sounds worse—have shaved their heads and raised the bar for all of us, public-display-of-concern-for-our-fellow-man-wise." I sigh.

My mom tents her fingers again. "So, it's all about who looks the most concerned?"

"No," I say. "It's about doing something helpful." I'm getting an idea here, so I keep talking. "It's about really connecting with your friend and doing something for him that shows you care about him. Something like, I don't know . . . I'm just thinking out loud here . . ." I glance over at Hector. I see his eyebrow twitch a little, which means he's plugged into my thinking.

". . . maybe we should shave our heads, too." Hector nods enthusiastically. My mom groans. Excellent. She shifts in the beanbag a little and glances at my dad.

"Well, you could shave your heads if that feels right to you," she says. "It's certainly a dramatic way to show your support for Tim . . . although Tim will not be losing his hair."

"That's a good point," I agree. "And you're saying that just because baldness works for Pierce doesn't mean it necessarily works for everybody."

"I know it doesn't work for me," my dad chimes in.

"Look, Sara and D'ijon have found a way of being support- ive that doesn't involve hair mutilation," my mom adds, "and maybe you could, too."

"Yeah. You mean like helping Tim participate in something cool that he'll be missing . . . like a . . . a church service or a lecture . . . or maybe a concert," I add.

Hector snaps his fingers and goes, "Hey! Isn't Gingivitis playing here this Saturday night? Tim loves Gingivitis. Maybe we could see that show for Tim!"

My folks look at each other and my mom says skeptically, "For Tim?"

"Yeah. For Tim," I say, using my best anime eyes.

My mom and dad look at each other.

"We'll see," which is the same thing as "Yes, but we're going to make you jump through a few hoops first, mister, and you'll live to regret the whole episode if anything goes wrong."

Hector and I nod solemnly, straight faces hiding the rave going on inside our heads at the moment. It's a known fact that too much facial gladness is a red flag to parents that can cause them to cancel any event that may have accidentally caused happiness in their children. Mi amigo and I have been friends for a long time, so neither of us needs words or even eye contact to know what the other guy is thinking. We just continue to stare blankly ahead, mentally congratulating each other.

Permission almost granted. Things are looking up. For Tim, I mean.

CHAPTER 7

I don't know about anybody else, but when I wake up on a Sunday, I like to do it at my own pace. Like right this minute: I'm considering opening my eyes, but then I start piling up reasons to just go back to sleep.

Then the sun finds an opening in my improvised pizza box

window shade and starts grinding hot daylight through the back of my skull. I try to insulate myself by sandwiching my head between two pillows, but then the mattress starts to feel kind of lumpy, so I sit up and stretch a little. I hear a couple of little mouse-size knocks on my door, and my mom pokes her head in my room.

"Yoo-hoo! Are you in th— Jeremy! Don't tell me that you just got up!"

"Okay." I yawn. "I won't. By the way, this mattress sucks." She just stares at me for a second, then she points to the other side of the room.

"Oh. Well, in that case, the stuff on my floor that I've been sleeping on all week sucks." She sighs and drops a stack of clean underwear next to me and turns to leave. I lie down on them and notice an immediate improvement in the sleeping surface. Over her shoulder my mom says, "By the way, I saw Sara and her mom at the farmers' market this morning and she said to remind you that you were supposed to call her."

I grab my phone and scroll through my recent messages, and there it is. At 1:47 a.m. I sleep texted Sara, "Happy Sunday. Let's hang out this p.m. Call you first thing with an amazing idea." Great. I should not be allowed to sleep and text. But oh, well . . . since I do my best work under pressure, I punch her number and start thinking of great ideas as it's ringing. Being spontaneous is my trademark. My dad calls it

My mom calls it

My mind is ripping through a million ideas for stuff to do tonight when I hear, "Hi, Jeremy," and everything shuts down. There's something about Sara's voice and the way she talks that just blows me away. Every idea I might have had or ever will have just leaves my head. "Hey," I finally say. "Hi. I was just, umm, calling to tell you my, uhh, great idea for, uhh, tonight, and, umm . . ."

"I can't."

"Yeah . . . I'm babysitting."

"You are?"

"Yup. Until ten. I'll just be mostly sitting there with nothing to do and nobody to talk to at six thirty-nine Windmill Lane. It's a light gray house with a big, comfy couch and a kid who goes to bed at eight."

"Oh," I say.

Then I get the World's Greatest Idea. "Hey! Maybe I could come over and see you at your babysitting job!" Sara sighs. . . . That's a good sign, right?

"Okay. I gotta go. I'll see you tonight!" I hang up before she can say no. Babysitting means responsibility, responsibility means boredom, and boredom leads to making out. "Huhhhhh . . ." I blow into my hand, take a deep sniff, and the room starts to spin.

Time to disinfect.

After a nice, long shower I'm in a pretty good mood. I try to shower when my dad is at work because he's always yelling about the water bill whenever I'm in there for more than an hour or two. Whatever. It's time to focus on the details.

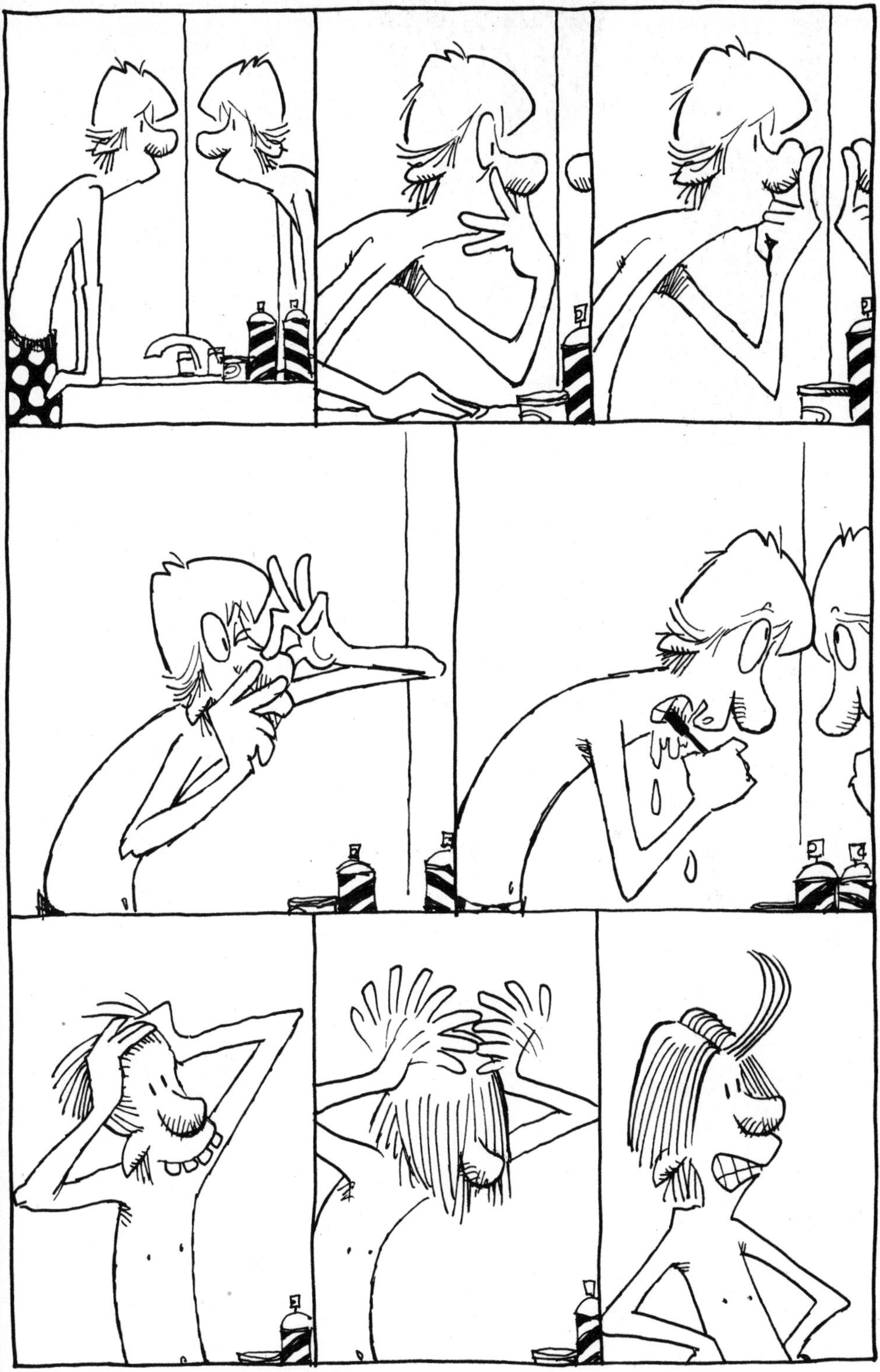

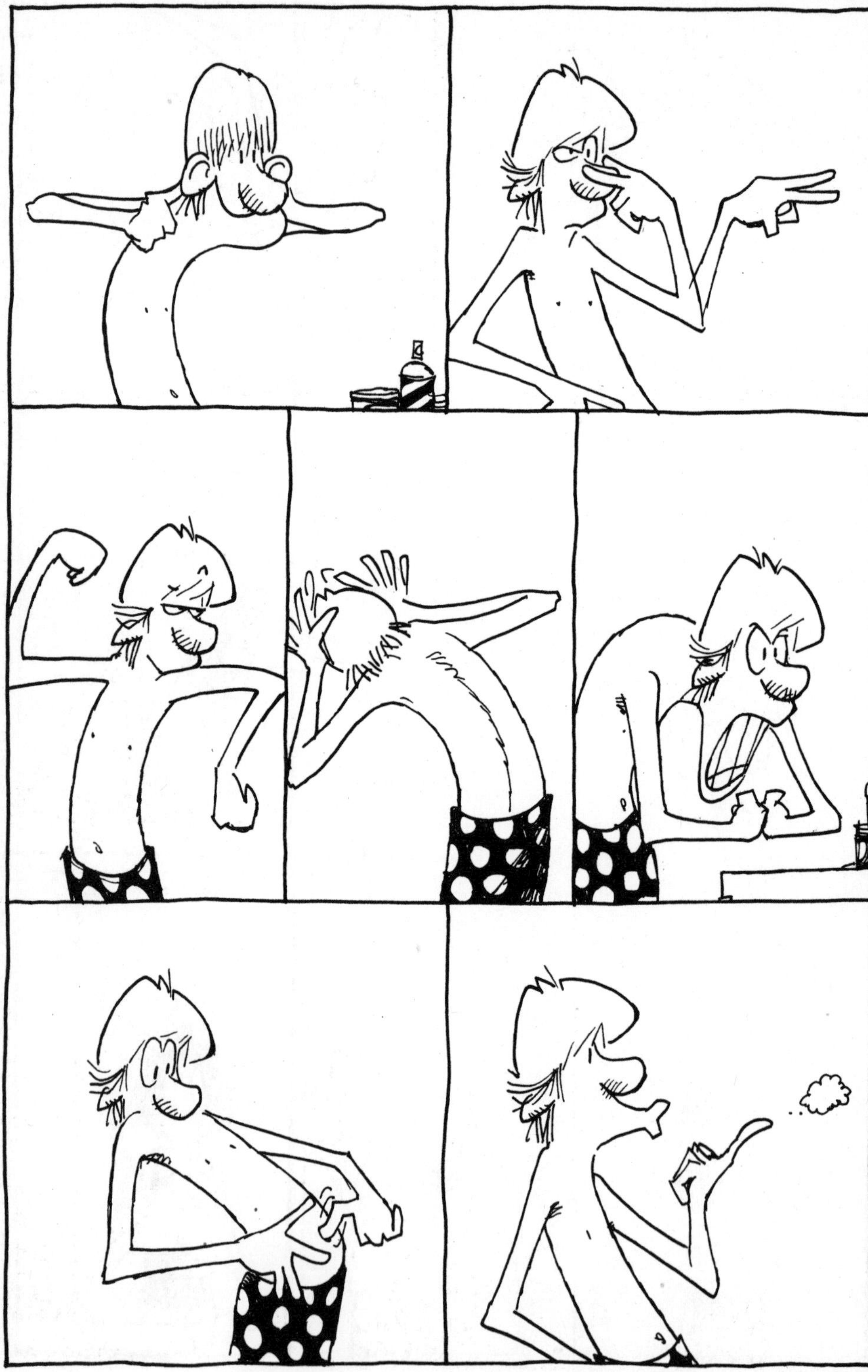

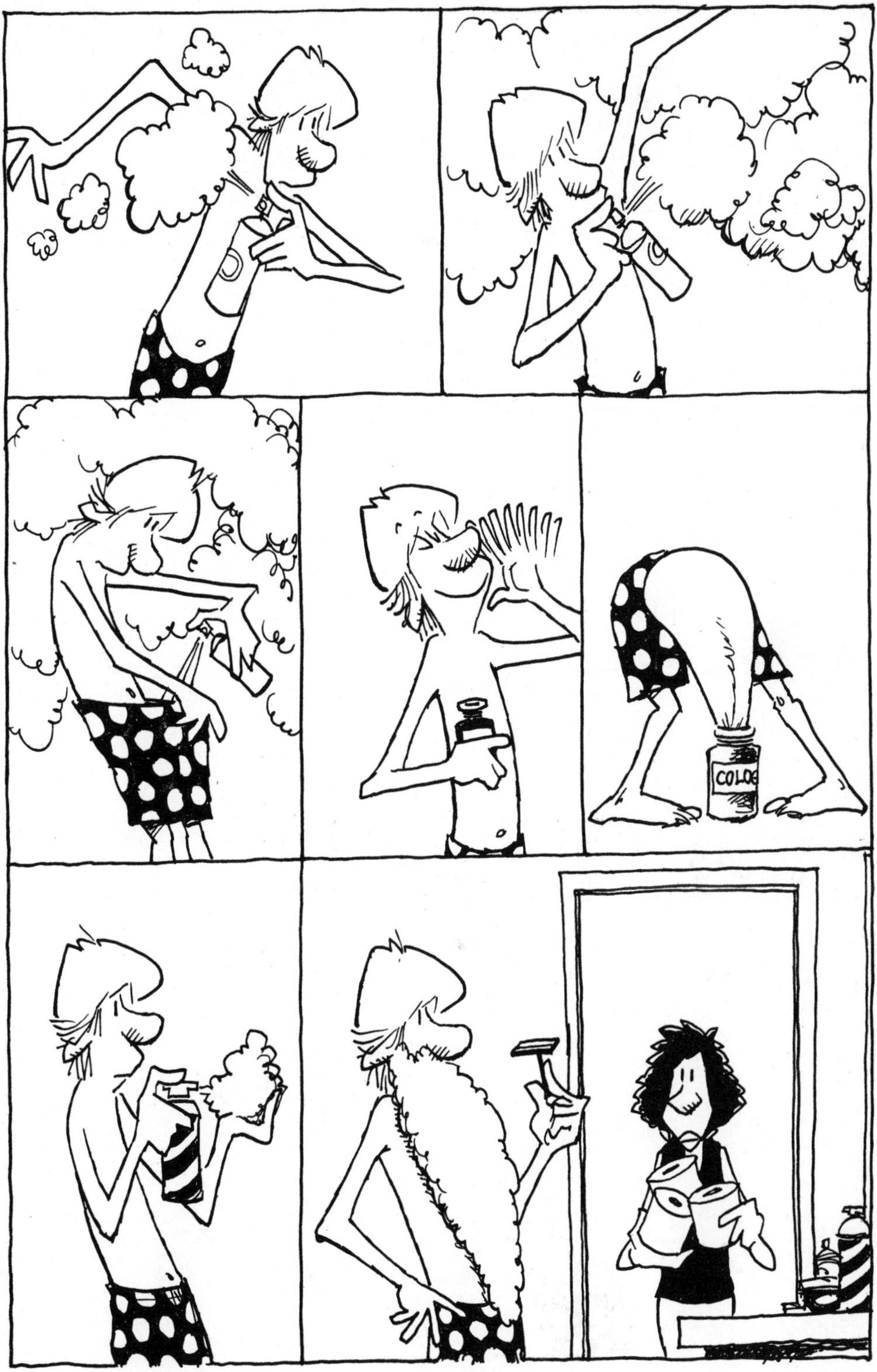
COLOG

"Oh, excuse me, Jeremy. I didn't know you were still in h—
What *are* you doing still in here?" My mom is always barging
in on me in the bathroom with flimsy excuses like restock-
ing the toilet paper or bringing me fresh towels. "Weren't you
going to take a shower, like, an hour ago?"

"Something like that," I answer. She tosses the empty toilet paper roll in the trash and starts to snicker to herself as
she folds a fancy fan-shape thing on the end of the first sheet.
She does this every time and thinks it's hilarious. Something
about the contrast between chaos and elegance cracks her up,
I guess. I turn sideways and look at myself in the mirror. My
ribs stick out so much it looks like I have a xylophone implant.

"This is unbelievable. I try really hard, but I cannot manage
to put on any weight."

HOW DO YOU DO IT, MOM?

Several hours and about a dozen getting-even-for-that-comment-about-the-size-of-my-mom's-butt chores later, I'm cruising the van down Windmill Lane, looking for the place where Sara is babysitting. It's getting dark and I can barely read any of the house numbers, so it's not really my fault that I knock over a garbage can as I pull up in front of 639. People should be more courteous.

Sara opens the door and I see this little kid—a girl, I think—wrapped around her legs.

"I'm here," I say.

"We know," says the kid. "We smelled your aftershave about ten minutes ago, stinky."

Yeah. It's a girl.

"For your information, it's not aftershave, kid. It's body spray. And I didn't even use that much this time." They both just look at me. "Okay, I did, but it's not my fault that the stupid nozzle stuck. What was I supposed to do, just spray it into the ozone or something? I have a conscience, you know." Then the kid just grabs my hand and pulls me inside.

"C'mon. It's your turn."

I am sixteen years old, and I want to make it clear that this is the first time in my life that I have ever had my toe-nails painted. It's not completely unpleasant, but it's definitely weird, and the only way Sara could get the kid to promise to hit the sack by eight. Nine down, one to go.

"Last toe, then it's bedtime, Kayla," says Sara.

"Toes, then hair, *then* bed. Remember?"

This kid is a real negotiator. She'll probably have her law degree by middle school.

"I didn't say you could definitely style Jeremy's hair, Kayla. I said we would have to ask Jeremy if it's okay with him." Kayla looks up at Sara and then at me.

"I think it's okay with him. Cuz if it's not, I might have a really hard time staying in bed until my mommy and daddy get home."

Impressive. I didn't learn to blackmail babysitters until I was at least ten. The kid and I lock eyes in a poker stare, and in about three seconds I can tell she's not bluffing. The message is clear: No hair styling for her, no quiet time for Sara and me. Take it or leave it. I shrug, set the alarm on my phone, then shake hands with the runt.

"You have ten minutes."

Nine minutes later—yeah, I swindled the little swindler—my phone alarm beeps and Sara hauls the kid off to bed.

"Good night, Jeremy."

"See ya, Kayla. Thanks for all the, um, beauty and stuff."

"No problem. Next time we'll do dress up."

Yeah, like that's ever going to happen. Sorry, kid, but I have my limits. A guy's gotta draw the line somewhere to protect his manliness.

After my toenails have finally dried and the kid is in bed, Sara plops down next to me on the couch and starts texting. That's weird. I thought she wanted me to come over here so we could make out, but that vibe is not happening. I turn my phone camera on myself. Everything looks okay . . . no residual curlers in my hair or Hello Kitty stickers on my face. Now I have to find a way to ask her if she's mad at me or something. I decide on the direct route.

"Are you mad at me or something?"

"No," she says, without looking up from her Very Important Text. Okay, that's a good sign.

"*Annoyed* might be a better word for it." Not a good sign.

"What did I do?"

"It's more what you didn't do. You were so sweet to Kayla just now but so unhelpful to Tim yesterday. Pierce was the only one who actually did anything at all. Jeremy, when Tim was needing support from his best buds, you just stood there and looked at him."

"I did?"

"Yes! And you didn't even ask him if he needed anything!"

"I didn't?" Sara pushes Send, tosses her phone down between us, and folds her arms across her chest. This is not going well. I start thinking about just leaving when something weird happens. For no good reason, I remember what my dad said to me the other day when he was cleaning the barbecue. "Women and girls thrive on connection. If you open up and share what's really inside you, all the other little spats and quarrels will evaporate."

Whoa. That might just be crazy enough to work. Something's definitely going on with Sara, so I nudge her freckled shoulder with my elbow and in my best understanding-yet-testosterone-soaked voice say, "Hey. Sorry. Wanna talk about it? I mean really?" She looks at me for a second, then takes a deep breath (removing most of the oxygen from the room) and says:

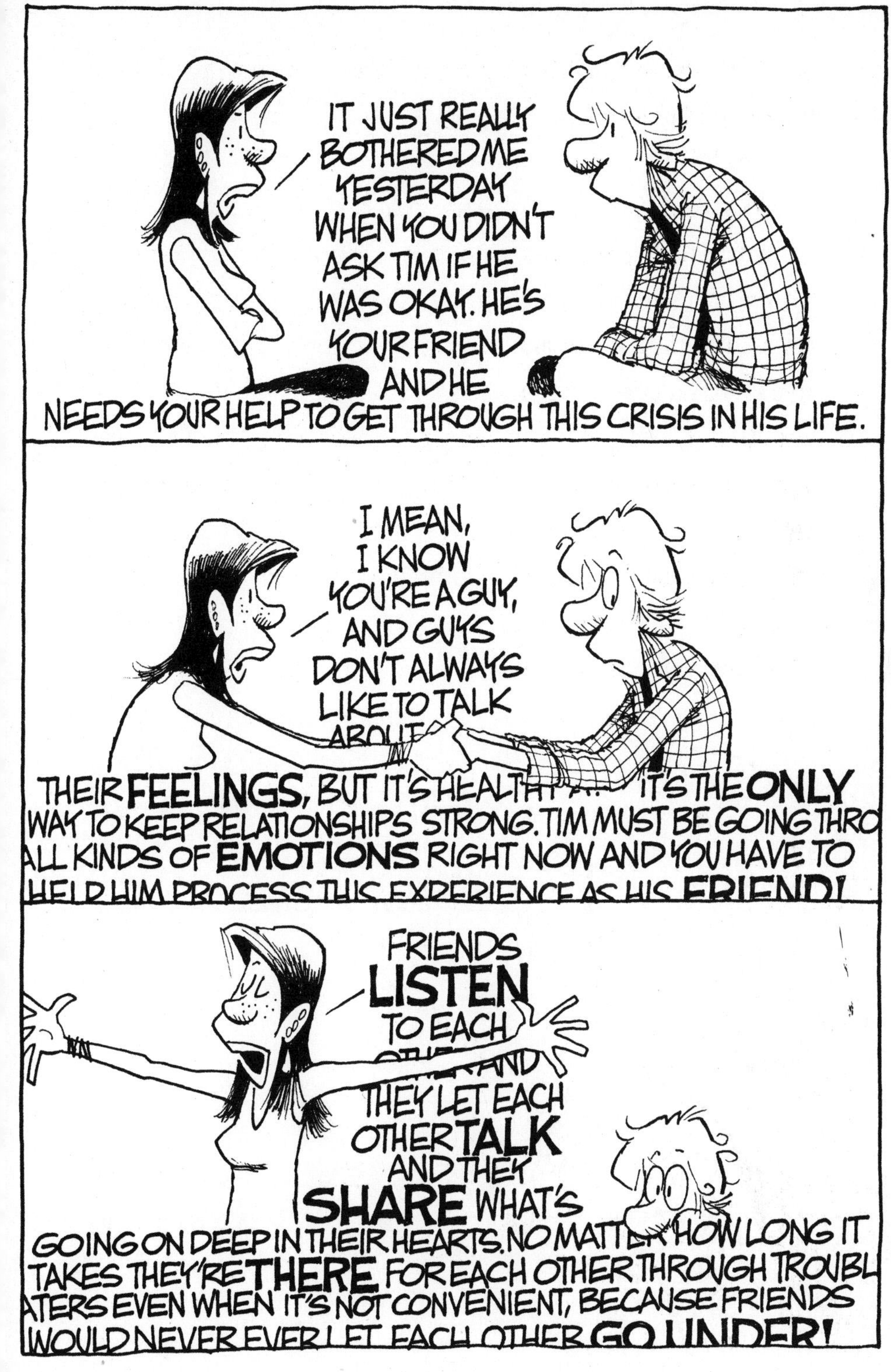
IT JUST REALLY BOTHERED ME YESTERDAY WHEN YOU DIDN'T ASK TIM IF HE WAS OKAY. HE'S YOUR FRIEND AND HE NEEDS YOUR HELP TO GET THROUGH THIS CRISIS IN HIS LIFE.
I MEAN, I KNOW YOU'RE A GUY, AND GUYS DON'T ALWAYS LIKE TO TALK
THEIR **FEELINGS,** BUT IT'S
IT'S THE **ONLY** WAY TO KEEP RELATIONSHIPS STRONG. TIM MUST BE GOING THRO
ALL KINDS OF **EMOTIONS** RIGHT NOW AND YOU HAVE TO
HELP HIM PROCESS THIS EXPERIENCE AS HIS **FRIEND!**
FRIENDS **LISTEN** TO EACH
AND
THEY LET EACH OTHER **TALK** AND THEY **SHARE** WHAT'S GOING ON DEEP IN THEIR HEARTS. NO MATTER HOW LONG IT TAKES THEY'RE **THERE** FOR EACH OTHER THROUGH TROUBL
ATERS EVEN WHEN IT'S NOT CONVENIENT, BECAUSE FRIENDS WOULD NEVER EVER LET EACH OTHER **GO UNDER!**

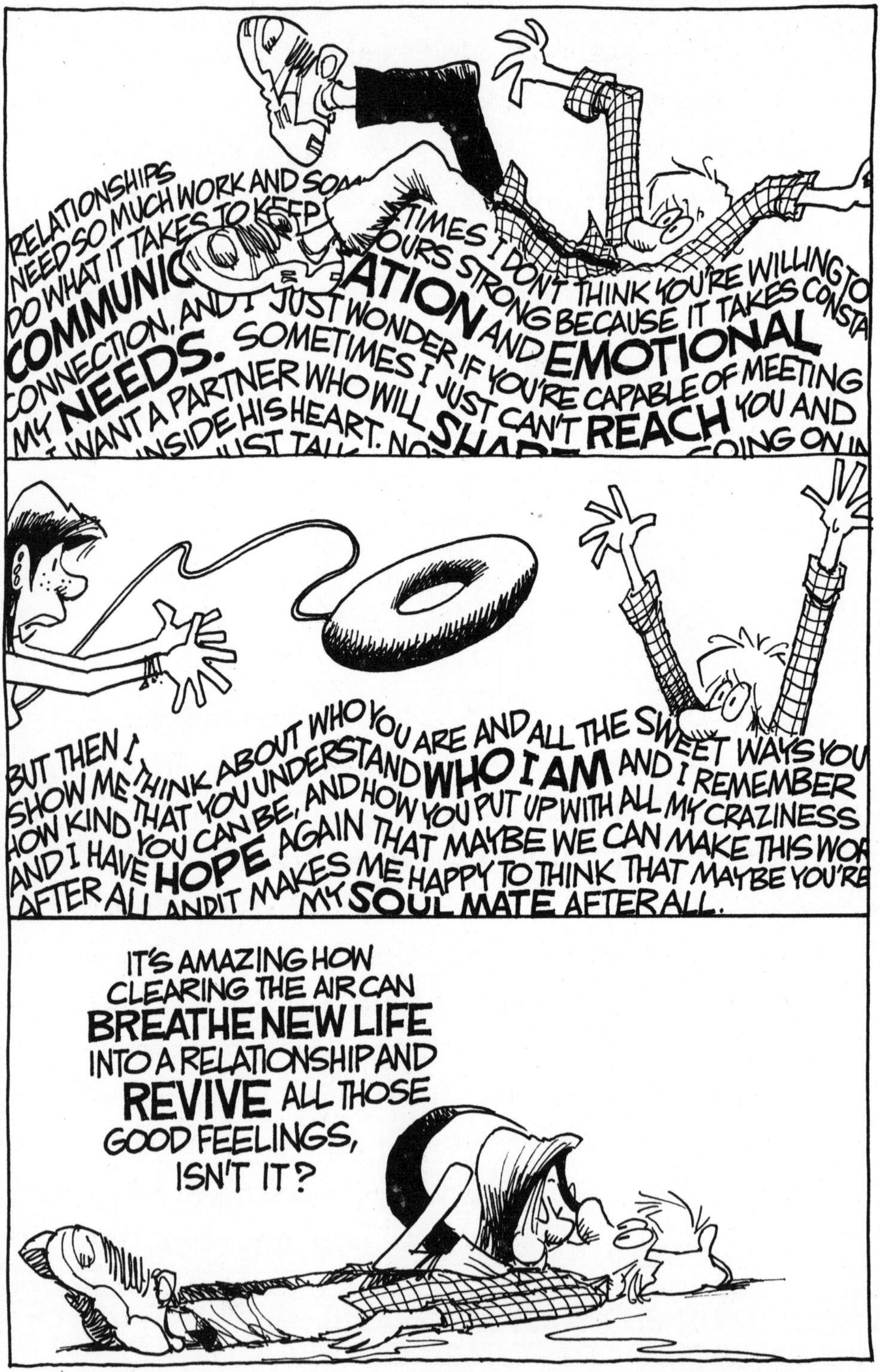
RELATIONSHIPS
NEED SO MUCH WORK AND SO
DO WHAT IT TAKES TO KEEP
TIMES I DON'T THINK YOU'RE WILLING TO
YOURS STRONG BECAUSE IT TAKES CONSTA
COMMUNIC ATION AND EMOTIONAL
CONNECTION. AND I JUST WONDER IF YOU'RE CAPABLE OF MEETING
MY NEEDS. SOMETIMES I JUST CAN'T REACH YOU AND
I WANT A PARTNER WHO WILL
INSIDE HIS HEART.
BUT THEN I THINK ABOUT WHO YOU ARE AND ALL THE SWEET WAYS YOU
SHOW ME THAT YOU UNDERSTAND WHO I AM AND I REMEMBER
HOW KIND YOU CAN BE, AND HOW YOU PUT UP WITH ALL MY CRAZINESS
AND I HAVE HOPE AGAIN THAT MAYBE WE CAN MAKE THIS WOR
AFTER ALL AND IT MAKES ME HAPPY TO THINK THAT MAYBE YOU'RE
MY SOUL MATE AFTER ALL.
IT'S AMAZING HOW CLEARING THE AIR CAN BREATHE NEW LIFE INTO A RELATIONSHIP AND REVIVE ALL THOSE GOOD FEELINGS, ISN'T IT?

We sit there looking at each other and she smiles.

"It feels good to talk. Thanks for asking."

"You're welcome," I say. She moves her phone over to the arm of the couch and scoots in really close to me. With her lips barely brushing mine, she whispers, "And I still want to make out with you, even though you have purple toenails." This is awesome! I guess my dad was actually right about something . . . but please don't quote me on that. And then Sara's phone alarm goes off. All the talking and listening has used up our make-out time, and the people she's babysitting for are due home soon. Ten seconds later I'm standing on the porch with my shoes in my hand and unintentionally wavy hair, realizing that even my dad's good advice can be annoying.

"One! Two! Three! Four!" Somewhere behind me a drummer—at least I think it's a drummer—counts off a beat and I lay into a tune that I'm totally making up as I play it. Of course I sound incredible, and the fans are going nuts. Even though the stadium is huge, I can feel the hot breath of the salivating crowd of fifty thousand hungry dogs who are hanging on to every note coming from my meat guitar. The stage lights cook the top of my head as my fingers fly up and down the greasy bacon neck of the instrument. I don't think I've ever played an edible guitar, but it feels totally natural, and it smells like breakfast. The crowd is going nuts as I just shred my solo. A chant rises, softly at first, from high in the upper deck. "Rer-em-y! Rer-em-y! Re-rem-y!" Then some guy in the front row clears his throat and puts his hand on my shoulder and I open my eyes a crack.

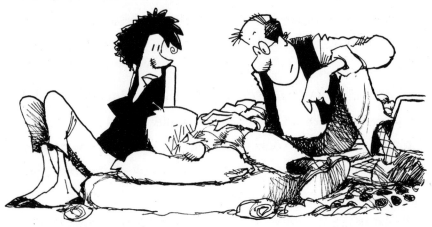

"Oh. Hi, Dad." The music and the meat guitar start to make a little more sense to me as the dream fades. Morning. Bacon. Duh.

"Hey, son. Got a minute?"

"Um, yeah. I guess so. What's up?" My mom starts rubbing my back like she used to do when I was a little kid. Creepy. Either somebody died, or we're moving to Spokane. My dad takes off his glasses and starts cleaning them with the end of my sheet.

"Your mother and I have been talking, and we want you to know that we've noticed some mature behavior on your part."

I start to protest but then remember that mature is a good thing in their book. "Like what?" I ask. Man, this is getting even weirder than my dream. Now he's rubbing his glasses even harder with the sheet.

"Well, your grades have been good, and you have started

hand washing your athletic cup like we asked you to, instead of putting it in the dishwasher . . . but the big thing is that you're trying to support your friend Tim instead of backing away. That makes us really proud. A lot of adults I know could learn something from you."

My dad holds his glasses up to the light and squints through them. The lenses are practically opaque.

"Plus, you didn't just run upstairs and shave your head like Pierce did. That shows r— When was the last time you washed these sheets?"

"I don't know," I say, because I don't. "What's your point?"

My dad hands the glasses to my mom, and she starts wiping them with the end of her T-shirt as she chimes in. "Our point is that we think it's admirable that you want to do something for Tim, and we want to help make it happen."

THIS IS STARTING TO GET INTERESTING!

"I'm listening." My mom holds the glasses up and squints through them. No improvement. Maybe I *should* think about washing these sheets.

"Oh, for Pete's sake," she says. "I'm going to go get the Windex." Then she stands up, which sort of throws my dad off balance a little, and he kind of falls over onto my laptop. As he rolls off it (thank God for AppleCare) and onto the floor, my mom puts her hands on her hips and says, "Look, we know that you already bought the Gingivitis tickets. And even though we're not happy about that, it's done." I look up and see that her gaze is set on full stink eye, and her voice drops to an ominous growl. "You say you want to go to this concert *for Tim.'* Well then, we expect you to come up with a way to do exactly that, Mother Teresa."

"How did you know about the tickets?" I ask. She cocks her head and gives me that "don't mess with me" look. "Please. I'm your mother. I know things about you that you don't even know yet." She reaches down and helps pull my dad up to his feet. After they're both gone, she sticks her head around the door and hisses:

The door closes.

"Oh."

"My."

"God."

I reach for my phone. Where is it? I dive under the covers, searching. Nothing! Oh, wait. It's in my hand. I speed-dial Hector, and he answers on the first ring.

"Yo."

"Dude! My parents just said that I can go to the concert!"

"Excellent," he says.

"Now all we have to do is come up with a plan for you to get permission from your folks."

"I think I have one."

"It has to be at least as brilliant as the one I used, and the key is going to be convincing them that I am a responsible and mature enough person for you to go with."

"Okay," he agrees.

For a minute I hear what sounds like muffled laughter and high fives, and then Hector comes back on the phone.

"I can go."

CHAPTER 8

Hector twists the volume down on our one working speaker and looks at me.

"We missed the turn again, dude." Then he amps the music back up and starts laughing, so I start laughing and neither of us can remember having this much fun on a Saturday night. Ever. I pull into the Taco Bell parking lot so I can try again. For a second I think about getting something to eat, but we've already stopped here twice for food so it would probably seem weird. I decide to wait until we find our seats and can check out the concession stand. As I circle the building, past the drive-through lane I'm hit by the ginormity of it all.

"Hector, we are on our way to an actual Gingivitis concert!" I yell, pounding the wheel.

"Fourth time's a charm." And then I howl like an idiot as I slip into traffic and head back toward the intersection. This time I actually get into the turn lane. Hector clicks the iPod to "Chain Saw Lullaby," and right on the downbeat the light changes and—wait, no cars are moving. We just sit there, and it stays that way through three more green lights. A traffic jam on the night of a concert? I did not see that one coming. We finally start inching forward, and for what seems like twenty minutes we go exactly one block. When we get near the front of the line where everybody is turning into a parking lot, Hector gasps.

"Ten bucks for parking??" he yells. "Are you kidding me?

What a rip-off!" This is not good. We scrounged all the money we had and brought it with us so we could buy an amazing cool Gingivitis souvenir for Tim, namely one of their signature leather jackets with fringe along the sleeves and the band's logo hand-tooled on the back. That's our idea for helping Tim. Having a mom with cancer is bad, but having a mom with cancer and a totally cool leather jacket would at least be a little less bad. Even my mom kind of agreed that it was a brilliant idea.

Hector yells, "Pull out of line! I think I know a place we can park for free." I yank the wheel to the left and we stutter off the shoulder and back onto the street. We hear a pretty loud rattle, like something might be coming loose from the van, but neither of us can see anything lying in the street behind us. Stuff is always falling off this machine, but we find that most of it isn't necessary anyway. If anything, the van goes faster without the extra weight.

Hector is navigating with his DQ Finder app. Okay, it's not exactly Google Maps, but the guy knows his fast-food joints and has the city mentally mapped out by their locations. He's like the Magellan of the Dilly Bar.

"It's not that far," Hector says. "I parked there during a triple chili dog event for seven hours one Saturday, and nobody said anything. We can walk For Tim."

"For Tim," I say, and return a fist bump. My phone starts vibrating and Hector grabs it for me.

"Sara's texting you."

"What's it say?"

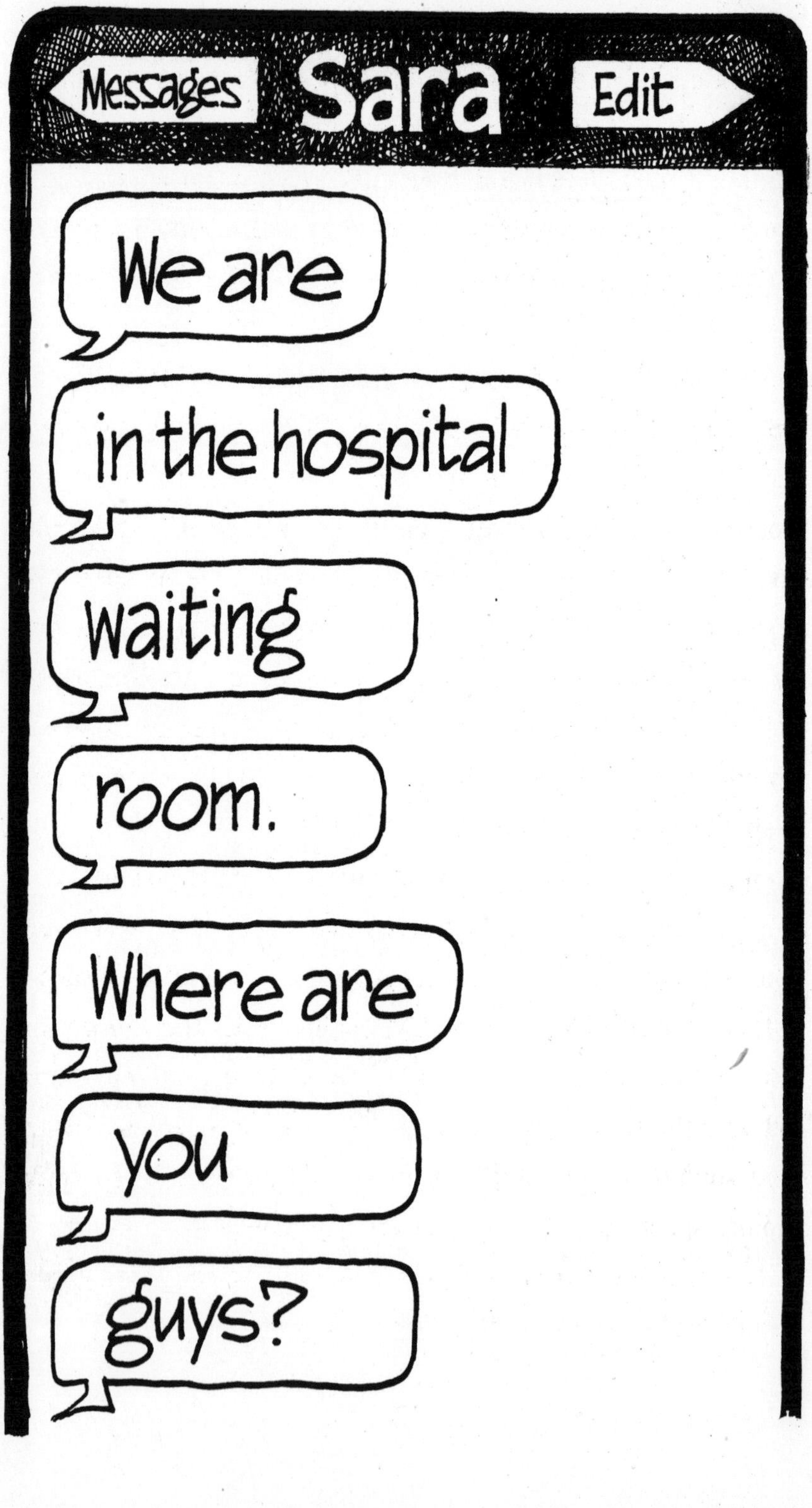
Messages
Sara
Edit
We are
in the hospital
waiting
room.
Where are
you
guys?

"Dude! You're being Shatnered!" This is something Sara and I do just to drive each other crazy. You send a text, but you break it up into a bunch of one- and two-word messages so that it reads like William Shatner talks in those jerky little word combos. She knows that if she does it long enough, it freezes my phone and I have to restart it. Is it any wonder that I'm in love?

We're at least eleven blocks from the arena when I finally spot a place to park. It's a crappy old home improvement center, like a prehistoric Home Depot or something. There are some cars scattered around the lot, so I'm sure it's okay for us to pull in . . . pretty sure, anyway. Most of the other cars look like they've been here for a while, which we take to be a sign of security. I don't see the pothole until it's too late, and we hit it hard. There's a bigger than normal klunkish sound followed by some harsh clanging, but the van seems fine, so I pull into a spot close to the building and kill the engine.

Or, to be accurate, I turn the key to the off position, and we sit there for the next four minutes as the van pitches and shudders like it's about to cough up a hairball in the parking lot. Hector and I figure that it's best just to let the van work it out on its own—nobody offers help to a cat that's about to hurl all over the floor, right? You just deal with it after it's all over, and sometimes these things just fix themselves. The engine finally sputters out, and I peel off my flannel shirt. It's probably eighty degrees outside and it smells like rain. Conditions are favorable for extreme awesomeness.

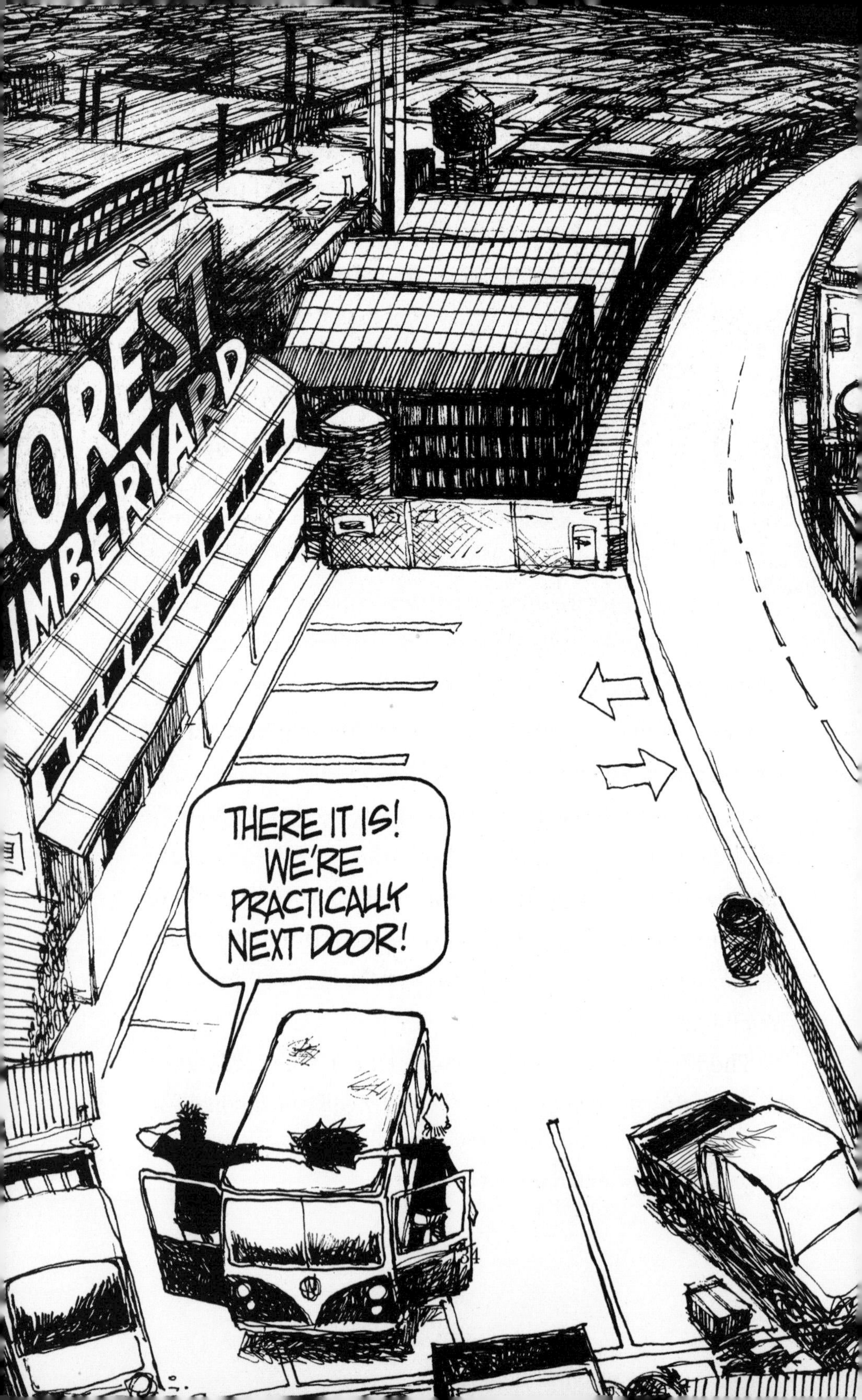
OREST
IMBERYARD
THERE IT IS! WE'RE PRACTICALLY NEXT DOOR!

For a minute the soft breeze blowing through a chain-link
fence and the buzzing of the flickering letters on the building's sign are the only sounds we hear. Well, those plus the
noise Hector's stomach is making as it processes the eleven
tacos he ate on the way. He lets out a huge belch that banks off
the glass doors and startles something in a Dumpster. I raise
an approving eyebrow. When it comes to gas, the dude's got
amplitude.

· The whole parking lot is bathed in the bile-colored glow of
the streetlamps, turning everything the color of zombie skin.
Perfect. It's semi-creepy and majorly cool. If this is freedom,
order me a case.

Hector and I look at each other across the roof of the van and I nod. "Let's do this." Hector grabs the bungee cord and hooks it through his door handle and hands me the other end. I wrap it around the steering wheel twice so it's nice and tight and hook the end under the brake pedal. The whole locking-up operation takes only a couple of minutes because we've done it so many times. Sure, it would be easier if we just got the door locks fixed, but this works, too. After all the doors are secured, we climb out through the hole in the roof and hit the ground running.

It's now exactly seven minutes before the warm-up band is supposed to start as we fall in at the back of the line of people waiting to get into the concert. There is just one word to describe this feeling—mindblowinglyepicallyawesome.

Hector and I are both dripping sweat from running all the way from where we parked, but it doesn't matter. In fact, it helps us blend in. I look around and silently greet My People. One of the weird things about being into a guitar mayhem band like Gingivitis is that it doesn't exactly place me among my peers. Our friends listen mostly to hip-hop, rap, and indie stuff, while the hard-core fans of rock are, well . . . older. And different. Like, Tim Burton different, okay? I don't think there's anybody here even close to our age, and if my mom were here she'd be Purelling every surface before she touched it. I couldn't be happier.

Just as Hector and I are clearing the turnstiles, the crowd noise swells a little and the warm-up band, Eat This Not That, backs into a semifamiliar tune and their one marginal hit, "Fried Oreo Hangover." This band's only job is to make Gingivitis look like rock behemoths by comparison, and so far they're (trust me) overshooting the target.

We trudge up about a thousand steps toward our high-altitude seats (thanks loads, Tim).

"Does the stage look small to you?" I ask Hector.

DUDE...

ANYTHING SMALLER THAN A DEATH STAR WOULD LOOK TINY FROM THIS DISTANCE.

I don't know why, but it didn't occur to me that row Z-Y might be above the tree line in this auditorium. On the hike up, we take in all the weirdos and burnouts in the crowd, especially the one guy way up there who looks like he's about to give himself an aneurysm. He's been jumping up and down and howling like an idiot. Seriously, get a grip, dude. It's a warm-up band. They have the same producer as the Wiggles, okay?

When Hector and I finally find our seats, there's an empty one to our left, which is great, considering it's the only place to put our knees. As we're sitting there, enjoying the lameness of the warm-up band and texting people about what an incredible time we're having, Hector starts in on the bass player.

"This guy brings douchebaggery to a whole new level," he says out of the corner of his mouth.

"No kidding," I say. "Tim is better than he is, and Tim stinks."

Hector cracks up. I start to say something about the bass player's mom when we hear, "WOOOOOOOOO!"

We look over. No. Way. Here comes this fifty-year-old stoner in a Foghat T-shirt crab-walking down the row with his butt motorboating people's faces. He stops every two feet to pump his fist in the air and WOOOOOOO again. Dude. Controlled substances are controlled for a reason. I look at Hector, and

at the same time we both say, "It's the aneurysm guy!" I get a quick picture of him with my phone (awesome lock-screen photo!), and we have just enough time to rearrange our legs before he plops down in our empty seat, sloshing beer all over his T-shirt and soaking the ponytail of the guy who's sitting in front of him. Classic.

This outburst was either because the warm-up band finished its set or because of the cold beer running down his belly and into his boxers. Whatever. The important thing is that we're here to see Gingivitis and they're about to toast our white bread world. Even from our sucky seats behind the soundboard guy we can see the roadies mopping the stage with fire retardant, which means "any minute now."

I start stomping my feet in that DUM!

DUM! CLAP! rhythm, you know, to get everybody to join in. They don't, of course, and the stoner gives me this perturbed look and goes:

"Okay," I say, pretending to understand his ancient seventies language, and then sit down. I roll my eyes at Hector, who is literally quaking as he tries not to laugh. His eyes are watering, and I can tell that he has a mouthful of Mountain Dew. Before he can swallow, I lean in and say a little louder than necessary, "I never shoulda dropped that Hippie as a Second Language class."

There's something beautiful about causing somebody to spew a mouthful of soda by just saying something hilarious (unless, you know, you're in the row in front of that person). *Now* it's a party! And, believe me, I'm not taking this for granted. For a while—actually, up until a few hours ago—we weren't sure if we were even going to be here. There was some minor misunderstanding between my parents and me about some stupid household chore I forgot to do, like my trash job for the past seven months. My mom was all "You are *not* going to this concert until you take this trash out," and I was all "You don't understand," and my dad was all "That's it! No concert!" So we compromised and I did the trash.

Google "unfair"; you'll find a link to my life.

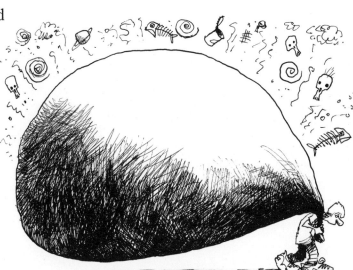

But that's in the past, and we're here and we are about to see guitar g—

—ods take command of the—

—arena crowd and just shred the place.

REALLY?

This arena is bigger, louder, and more awesome than anything I've seen. You can tell the place hosts circuses and monster truck rallies because my feet feel like they are cemented to the floor. I thought the movie theater was gross, but this floor has a much higher quality tundra of dried soda and cotton candy that has been compacted and polished to a high sheen. Awesome.

But, no worries. I brought binoculars and Gingivitis is in the building! You can feel the walls throbbing. This is Rock 'n' Roll! This is what I am about! For the first time in my life I feel totally free and independent!

And then it happens. The lights go down, and the crowd starts screaming. The sound is like nothing I've ever heard. It's like sitting inside a jet engine but in a good way. I look at Hector and see that he's screaming, and then I notice that my mouth is open and I'm screaming, too. Phones light up

everywhere in an amazing display of cellular solidarity as this deep voice says, "Ladies and gentlemen, please welco—" and the crowd drowns out the rest.

The stoner guy goes absolutely berserk. Hector is standing on the seat back in front of him with his arms in the air.
My mind leaves my body and looks down on us all in a full-on

hemorrhagefest of berserkitude. Gingivitis is playing like their hair is on fire . . . which it actually is for a second until a roadie snuffs it out with a blanket. They never miss a note.

Hector shoves the binoculars at me and screams what must be, "CHECK IT OUT!"

I scan around the stage and then scream back, "NO WAY!" I've been listening to Gingivitis since I was fifteen and I had no idea that the acoustic intro to "Quintuple Amputee" was plucked on Nigel's nipple studs. Unbelievable! I focus in on Nigel's left hand and wait. The chord in this song that I've

been trying to play is coming up, and this is my chance to see it done live. Gingivitis never plays a song the same way twice, so you never know when they'll throw in, say, an extended cowbell solo, like they're doing now. Bands do that so the lead singer has a chance to get a drink of water, have a smoke, make out with a groupie, or, in Nigel's case, all three. After about ten minutes, he strolls back onstage, slips his guitar strap over his shoulder, and nods to the drummer. Then just as they get to the stupid chord, Nigel turns to say something to the drummer and I miss it. Again. I'm bummed for about two seconds, but the "Big Wet Slobbering Kiss/ Do My Gums Look Infected?" mix pulls me out of it and I'm back in the moment.

When Ewan Ipswich tears into "Last Chance to Lick It" while riding a giant animatronic tongue, I just about spontaneously combust. There is no sound anymore, just white noise and the throb of twenty thousand screaming rock fans colliding with the gnarly howl of two million watts of guitar mayhem. I'm bouncing. I'm dancing. The music has taken over my entire being, and may have loosened my wisdom teeth, too. I feel like I'm floating on sound waves, and I never want to stop.

I punch Hector in the shoulder and mouth the words "Nothing in our lives will ever be the same!"

And Hector mouths back something that looks like "Yah dobbah okah jomba pok," so I nod. He shakes his head, points off to the side, and tries again. "YOU'RE! DANCING! ON! THE! JUMBO! TRON!"

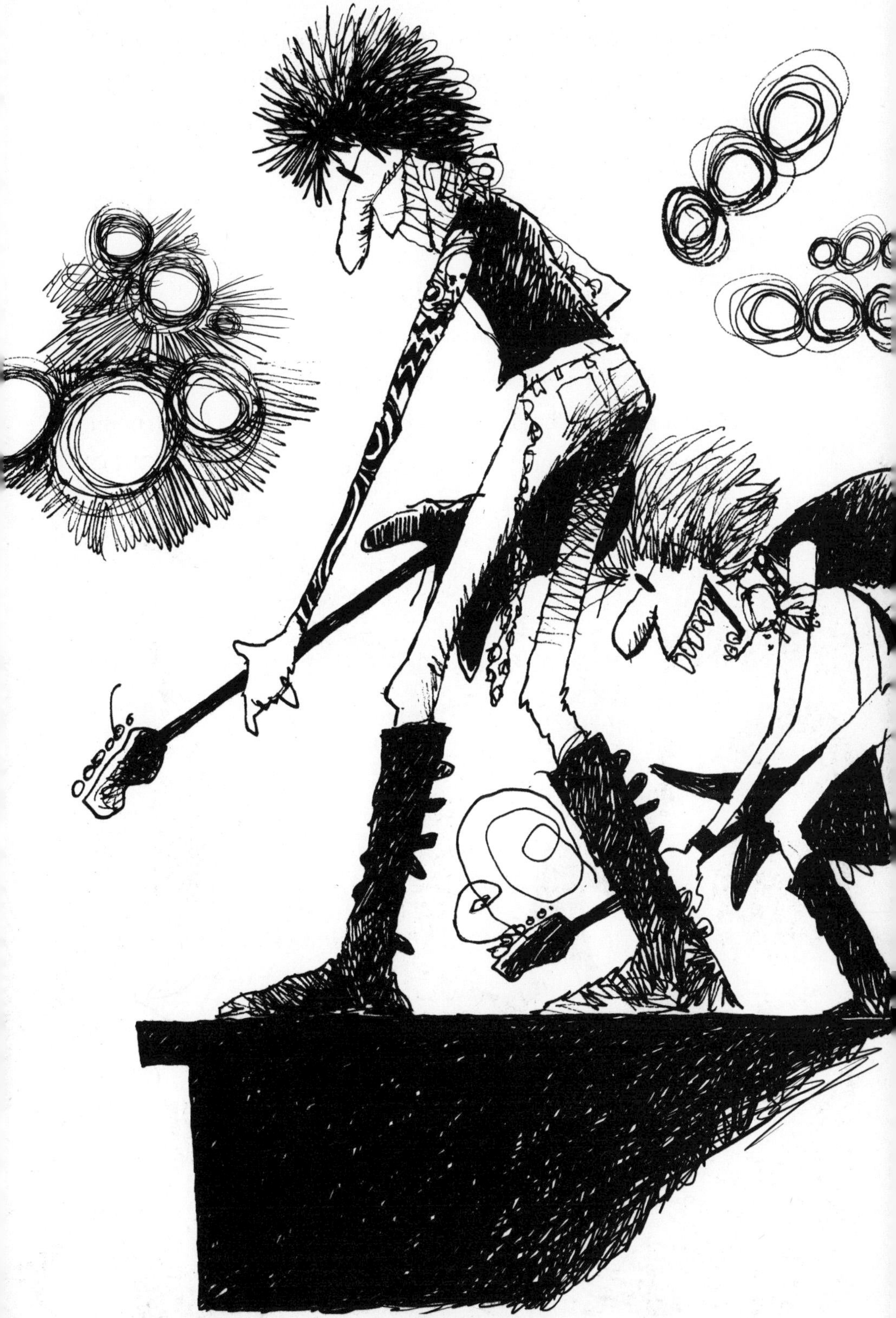

CHAPTER 9

Okay, this is bad. Zipper-down-during-science-report bad. Farting-at-a-funeral bad. Seniors-taping-your-underwear-to-your-locker-after-PE bad. It may even be worse than that time at a Reds game when I was caught sitting next to my mom on the kiss cam. Well, maybe not worse than that, but at least equal to it in sheer mortal humiliation. You know how time can seem to stop during traumatic events? Well, time has not only stopped, it is sitting down with its feet on the coffee table and eating a foot-long meatball sub while I've been on the Jumbotron.

As Ewan, Gingivitis's bass player, does one of those extended solos, and before I can find anybody else to blame, Nigel Mealsworth—ultimate rock god of the universe—points at me up on the huge screen and screams,

HEY! THAT KID LOOKS LIKE 'E'S MILKING A KANGAROO!

Yeah, that's good . . . now the three people in the arena who *didn't* see me looking like a complete tool have also been included in on the joke. The entire arena cracks up in a huge tsunami roar as Nigel leads the crowd through a gooning version of me dancing, and Hector and I ride the wave of mockery out of our section and into the cool, beer-soaked sanctuary of the cement tunnel behind the seats.

We skitter around like cockroaches in a flashlight beam while I pretend to be anybody else but me, but I finally tell Hector that I'll catch up with him at the concession stand and disappear into the end stall of the most remote men's room I can find. Eventually the urinal talk begins to change from "that goofy kid on the Jumbotron" to sports to cars to which band member looks the most wasted, and finally it feels safe to show my face again.

Or not. After that guy leaves I pretend to wash my hands, duck out the door, and my teeth immediately start vibrating. Maybe I wasn't hiding for as long as I thought because Ewan's bass solo is obviously still going on. A quick check of my phone and I can see that it's actually been thirty-seven minutes. If I had to bet on the most wasted band member, I'd put my money on him. But I have to find Hector, so I brush my hair down over my eyes a little and slide along the wall, scanning for a concession stand. It doesn't take long before I recognize Hector's hunched shoulders as he shoves a nasty plastic nacho tray into a trash can and wipes his mouth on his sleeve. He grins when he sees me and yells, "Dude!" About fourteen random guys turn around, thinking he's talking to them. Here's a free tip: Hollering "Dude!" at a rock concert is about as specific as yelling "Mom!" at a water aerobics class.

Hector kind of smiles, gives them the "never-mind" wave and then whispers to me, "Dude! You okay?"

"Besides miserable, I'm good," I say, pulling him around the corner. "We can watch the rest of the show after I regrow my cojones, but I think we should try to score Tim's jacket while it's relatively quiet back here."

"Excellent suggestion, amigo," Hector agrees as he shoves me forward with his shoulder. "There's a souvenir booth right up there, next to the beer stand."

"Hey, yeah! And there's the leather jacket!" I say, starting to jog. This is the win I needed. I start digging for the wad of bills in my front pocket, remembering how Hector and I pooled all our lawn-mowing money for this, and since we didn't have to pay for parking, we can spend every cent on the jacket for Tim. The line is only about four dudes deep, so Hector and I check out the merchandise as we're waiting. There are a couple of really cool shirts, especially the distressed one from the 2010 Mummified Rodent Parts tour. I could see that one working with jeans or even khakis and a sport coat if my parents were making me dress up for dinner or something.

A girl in the booth is actually wearing one of the Gingivitis leather jackets, and it's even cooler than I thought it was going to be. Every piece of the fringe on the sleeves has a little silver skull on the end of it, and when she moves, the skulls bang together like a demented wind chime. Hector and I look at each other and nod. This is definitely the thing that will help Tim get through this rough patch. I squeeze the money in my hand and wave the girl in the jacket over.

"Um," I say. "Just a second." Hector and I look at each other. He mouths "SEVEN HUNDRED FIFTY DOLLARS??" and I mouth "Holy!@*%!"

"Guys, is there something I can get you? Cuz there are other people in line here," the girl says. I turn around and try not to look as sick as I feel.

"Do you have anything for under forty-seven dollars and thirty-three cents, including tax?" I finally manage.

"Oh yeah! Sure," she chirps, and then reaches under the counter for a ratty-looking wooden box filled with little Gingivitis lapel pins, cheesy necklaces, neon glow sticks, miniature guitar straps, and an assortment of key chains. I point to the least pathetic key chain, shove some of our money at her and walk away.

If there's one thing worse than carrying around a stupid cheapo key chain when you thought you'd be scoring an awesome hand-tooled leather jacket featuring the official insignia of your favorite band, it's carrying said key chain in the arena where your personal idol in said all-time favorite band has just personally mocked you in front of ten thousand rabid fans on a high-definition Jumbotron. You can quote me on that. If I were a deeper person, I'd probably be ruined for life. As it is, I'll feel lousy for another ten minutes, and that'll be the end of it. One thing about us lightweights: we're resilient. Hector gives me a shoulder bump and says, "Chillax. Nobody has a decent attention span anymore. This is already forgotten." And that would have felt pretty good if at that exact moment we weren't passing by this group of people clustered around an iPhone and laughing hysterically at the YouTube video of me milking the kangaroo. One guy says that it's also posted on the Gingivitis website, and apparently a clip of me dancing in a third-grade play has gone viral. In my own defense, I'd like to point out that I did not volunteer for that play. Parts were assigned alphabetically, and all of us poor Duncans, Donaldsons, Duquettes, and Druckers were drafted into a chorus line of Fresh 'n' Healthy Dancing Veggies.

I sit down on a plastic chair and stare at Tim's crappo key chain. One side of it has last year's tour logo and the other side is blank. Great.

162

"Customers only in the seating areas, please!"

I catch a glint of light out of the corner of my eye, and then I look over at Hector. Where have we heard that overenunciated voice before? It's familiar, irritating, confident, and annoying all at the same time. And then it hits us.

When I was about six years old, I was at the grocery store with my mom and we saw my first-grade teacher in the cat food aisle. I remember it totally freaking me out to learn that teachers were allowed off school property. I always figured that they lived in the classroom and slept under their desks.

Now I'm equally freaked out to find my American History teacher serving beer to stoners and greasers at a rock concert.

Byczykowski asks the other bartender to cover for her and disappears behind the taps. Two seconds later she's pulling up a chair at our table with three Cokes and smiling that big, toothy smile of hers. "Good drinking crowd tonight. My bank account sure loves these headbanger concerts." The fluorescent lights reflect off her gold crowns, just like they do at school, and I'm instantly bored.

"Yeah," I say. I'm scanning my memory for conversation material involving the Battle of Antietam. I got nothing.

"It's insane in there," adds Hector. "Is this what you do for fun or something?"

She laughs and pulls her cap off and runs her hands through

her hair. I can see the sweat stains under her arms and she looks tired.

"Contrary to popular myth, high school teachers don't make a lot of money, guys. I have a friend who owns the concession here and he lets me work all the major events. I've been doing this for almost six years. It's hard work, but the tips make my Saturn payment, and . . ." She pulls a couple of marshmallow-size wads of cotton out of her ears,

She laughs, and we laugh, and suddenly it feels almost normalish to be sitting with her in public. "I saw you over at the souvenir booth a while ago. Did you get anything good?" Hector shuffles his feet and jams his hands into his pockets.

"If by 'good' you mean 'total-rip cheapo piece of crap,' then, yeah, we got something really good," he says.

"Oh," she says.

"Yeah." I sigh. "For Tim,"

Then for some reason we start to tell her the whole story about how we're supposed to be getting some amazing spirit-lifting memento from the concert for Tim because he's doing this bone-marrow-harvest thing tonight for his mom's cancer treatment, and all about the Jumbotron debacle, and the seven hundred fifty dollar leather jacket, and basically spilling our guts to our bartending American History teacher that, granted, makes no sense but, hey, what has tonight?

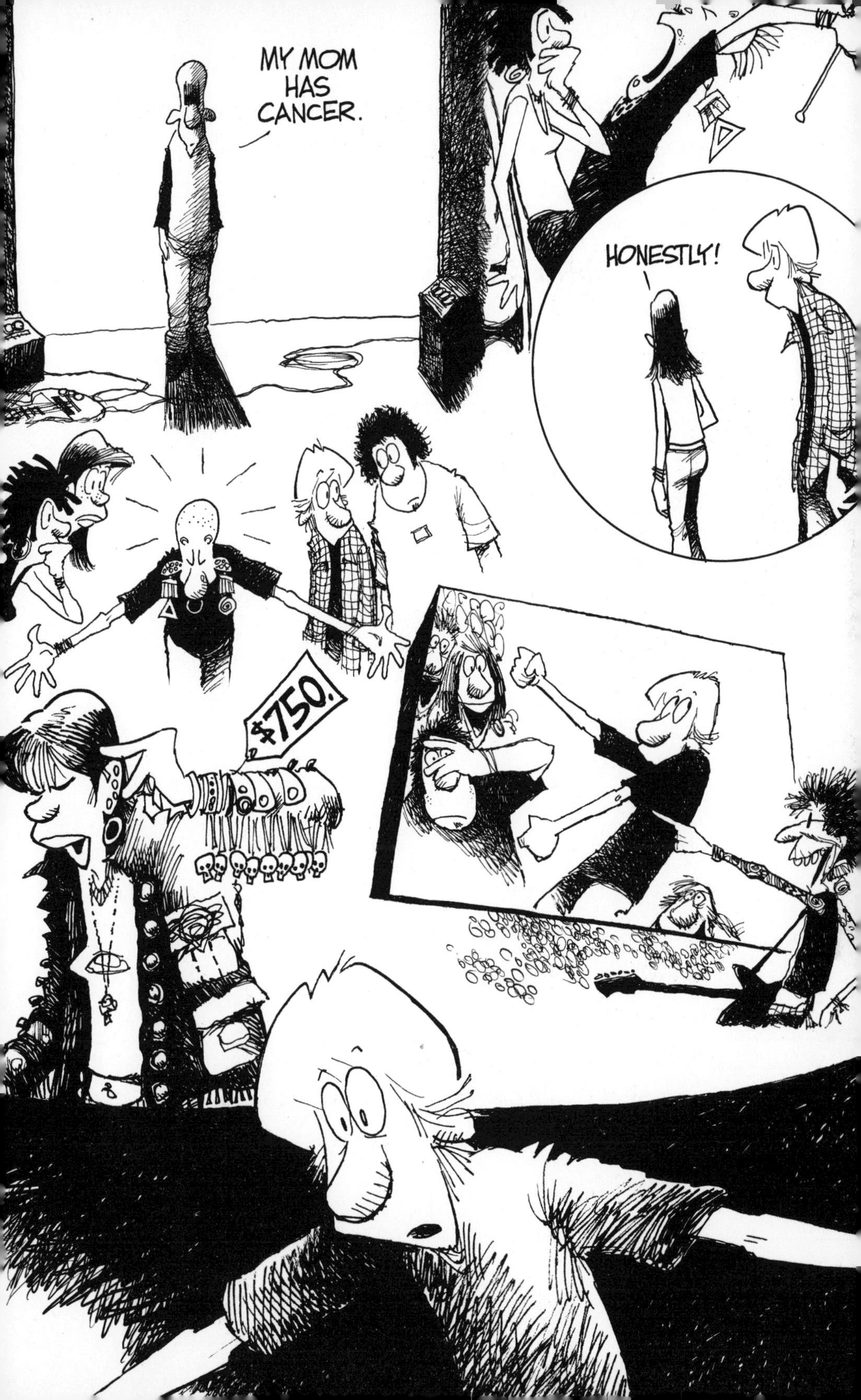
MY MOM HAS CANCER.
HONESTLY!
$750.

"Wow," Ms. Byczykowski says. Then she turns the key chain over in her fingers again and shrugs. "Well, at least the back side is blank so you could get it autographed."

"Yeah," Hector snorts. "All that would take is a backstage pass and a bucket of miracles."

There's a long pause as the distant strains of Nigel's intro to "Stapled Man Parts" echoes through the cavernous concrete tunnels around us. Great, a tearjerker. This is the first song I ever learned to play all the way through and the main reason my parents gave up on trying to make me play the clarinet.

I focus hard and will the tear in the corner of my eye back to wherever it came from. I've got this image in my head of my mom alone in a hospital room hooked up to IVs and I can't get it out. Damn it, I will not cry at a Gingivitis concert.

"Listen," says Ms. Bycz, and then she pauses again. "Maybe I can help you get backstage. But after that, you'll have to make your own miracles."

CHAPTER 10

If you don't count most of tonight, I'm a pretty lucky dude. I have parents who love me, plenty to eat, a roof over my head, and clothes under my feet. I have a hot girlfriend who hasn't figured out that I'm about half the guy she should be dating. And I have a best friend who catches on to a plan like lightning while I'm still staring into my Coke and feeling sorry for myself.

I hear some yelling coming from somewhere, but it barely

registers that something is happening until the pushing and shoving in the line next to us gets crazy and I'm splattered with beer foam. A skinny guy holding two huge cups of the stuff bangs into my chair, then yells,

Great. Draft beer and Axe body spray. Now I smell like about 90 percent of the guys here. It's the official scent of arena rock concerts. Gingivitis ought to bottle it and sell the stuff with their other crappy souvenirs. As I grab a fistful of napkins to start mopping up the suds in my ears, the guy who splattered me apologizes.

"Sorry, man. That dude back there is shoving everybody." I look back to where he's pointing and unsurprise! It's the obnoxious middle-aged stoner dude from the seat next to mine, now rowdier and even beerier than before. He's belly bumping everybody forward, trying to make the line move faster because he really needs more alcohol, the poor man. Personally, I'm not looking forward to reaching drinking age. I've tasted my dad's beer and, trust me, if it didn't give you a buzz you couldn't give that stuff away.

ONE SIP

BELCH!

FOO

TIMES TEN THOUSAND

Ms. Byczykowski lets out a low growl, and I can see her eyes are laser locked on the stoner dude like he's a sophomore with a counterfeit hall pass. Her upper lip curls slightly as she puts a couple of eight dollar beers on the counter and disappears through a door in the back of the stand. Two seconds later she's standing in the doorway with a case of plastic cups next to a small sign that says

Her head tilts about a thousandth of an inch toward the sign as she makes Meaningful Eye Contact with Hector. Hector sits up straight like a Doberman and I see his ear twitch. I think I can actually hear his brain engage in a higher gear.

"Got it," he says under his breath. His eyes narrow, and it slowly dawns on me that something is up. I may not be the tightest string on the Stratocaster, but I see what's going on here. Byczykowski is hatching a plan. I lean over and, without moving my lips, say, "I think our history teacher wants to make out with you in the storage room!"

Hector stares at me for a second with a "shut up and get ready, you idiot" look on his face, then whispers, "Shut up and get ready, you idiot."

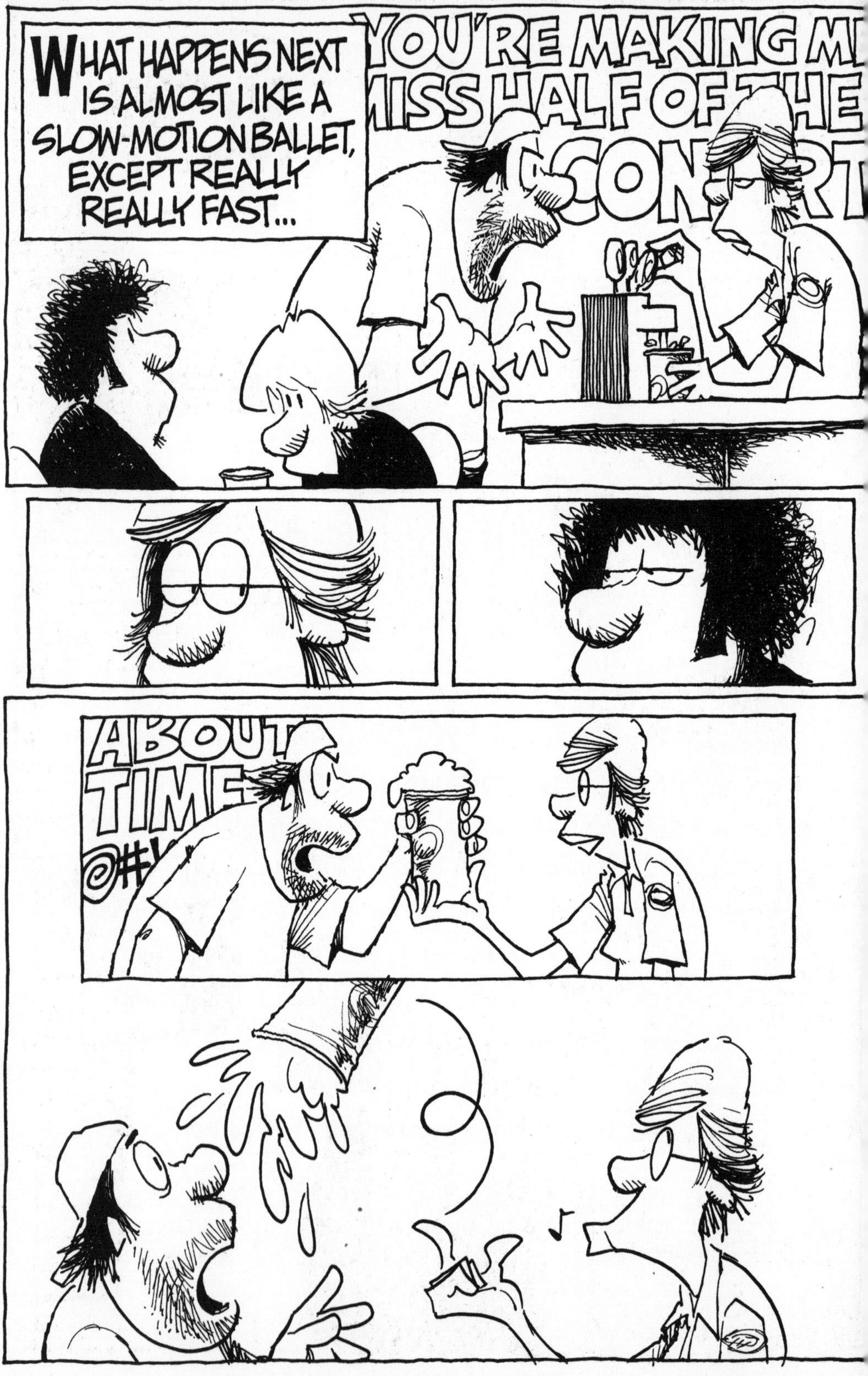
WHAT HAPPENS NEXT IS ALMOST LIKE A SLOW-MOTION BALLET, EXCEPT REALLY REALLY FAST...
YOU'RE MAKING M
MISS HALF OF
ABOUT
TIM

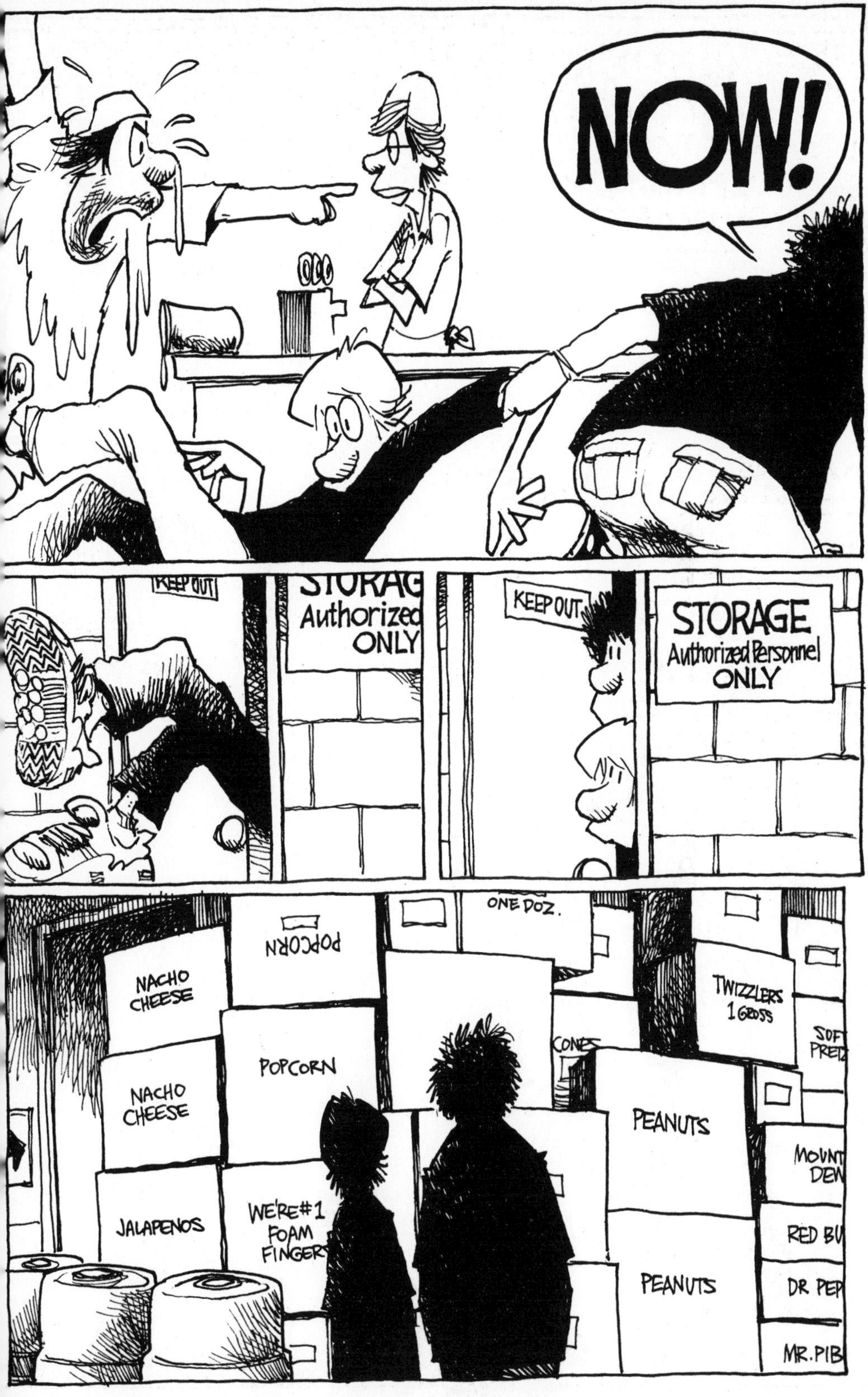
NOW!
KEEP OUT
STORAG
Authorized
ONLY
KEEP OUT
STORAGE
Authorized Personnel
ONLY
ONE DOZ.
POPCORN
NACHO CHEESE
TWIZZLERS 1 GROSS
CONES
POPCORN
NACHO CHEESE
PEANUTS
JALAPENOS
WE'RE #1 FOAM FINGERS
PEANUTS
RED BU
DR PEP
MR. PIB

I don't think anybody even noticed as Hector dragged me under the counter and into Byczykowski's storage room, because when we peek around the door, they're all out there slipping and sliding into a beery pileup in front of the booth. I can hear Ms. Bycz fake apologizing to the stoner dude as two massive security guys pull him up off the ground. Hector eases the door shut and we look around. We're in a small windowless fluorescent-lit room stacked high with boxes of cups, foam We're #1 fingers, popcorn boxes, and beer kegs. I'm thinking that it *would* have been a good make-out room, then Hector points toward a stack of Skittles boxes and whisper yells, "Check it out! A door!"

We shove the boxes out of the way and, sure enough, there's a steel door propped open just slightly with an empty eyeglass case bearing the image of Ulysses S. Grant.

"Whoaaaaa . . . I am totally doing all the extra credit questions on Byczykowski's quizzes from now on," whispers Hector.

"Even her glasses are full-on history nerd," I say. "Yet, somehow, she rocks."

The sign on the door says HIGH VOLTAGE, DO NOT ENTER and a couple of other things that don't really mean anything, so we open it and look down the long, darkish tunnel. It must lead backstage because we can hear the crowd screaming as Nigel finishes one of his buzz saw solos. I can almost smell melting guitar pick from here. I hear Hector swallow hard, then say, "Tim would do this for us, right?"

I shrug and take off at full speed with Hector pounding behind me. Our footsteps echo off the walls as we're propelled down the tunnel by the warning signs posted every twenty feet or so.

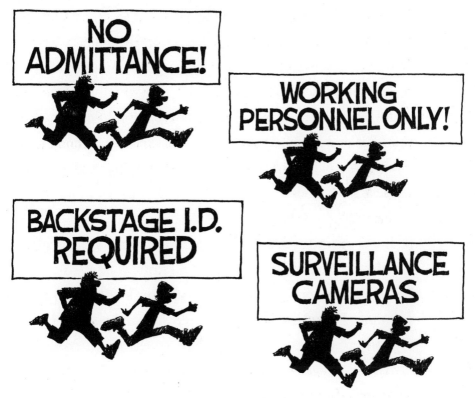

I know somebody probably put these up to scare people away, but they are having the opposite effect on me because I am pumped! But maybe not as pumped as Hector is, because he powers past me and disappears around a corner up ahead. I hear him yell back to me, "Dude! C'mon!" so I pick up the pace. When I duck around that same corner, I'm moving so fast that I run smack into a door with another big sign on it.

Anybody can see that this is an oxymoron, and I start to point that out to Hector, but the red light on the ceiling above me that just started flashing does seem to mean business, so we scramble for a corridor marked ELECTRICAL . . . don't ask me why.

I have no idea where we are, but we must be getting close to the stage because the music is getting louder. We duck under a chain and while we try to get our bearings, I recognize "Feral Carol," their platinum teenage anthem that closes every concert they play. The weird reverb from the tunnel actually improves the song, but this time they've overlaid it with squawking walkie-talkies and a thumping beat like a heart about to explode through a rib cage. Wait—those are separate sounds, and the last one is coming from my personal chest. The squawking is from actual walkie-talkies somewhere nearby.

"SKKXTT! Door fourteen is open. I'll have a look."

Hector and I look at each other and mouth "SECURITY!" I spot some metal steps and we climb for our lives.

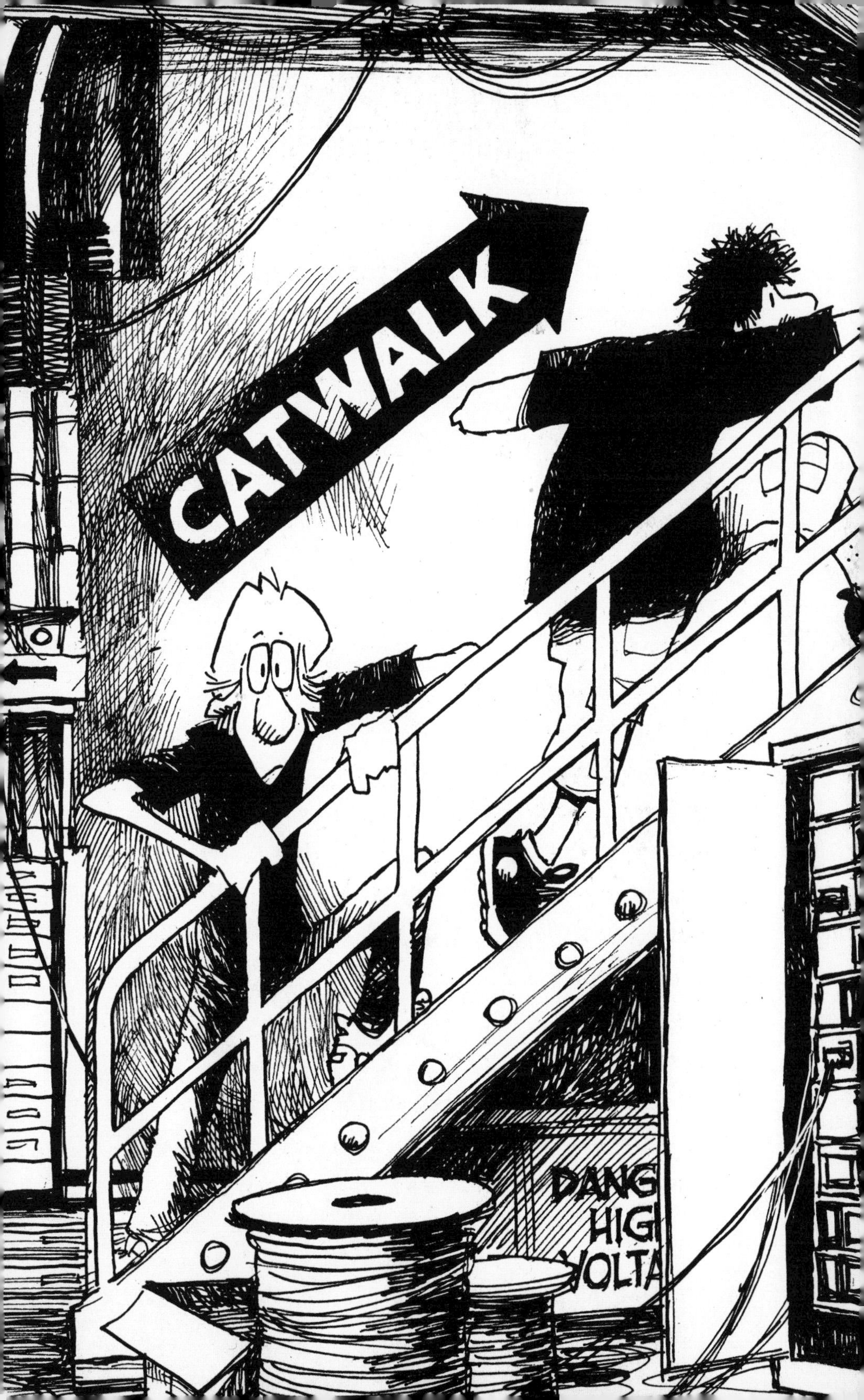
CATWALK
DANG
HIG
VOLTA

This staircase just keeps going! I feel like I've climbed, like, a thousand steps, but we can't stop because the walkie-talkies are right below us. My eyes are starting to adjust to the dark and I can start to see bundles of cables, ropes, counter-weights, and pulleys hanging everywhere. Hey! I read about this! We are in the middle of the fly system the crew uses

to move the sets around during the concert. I grab Hector by the back of his shirt and point to Nigel Mealsworth's actual stage tongue hanging, like, two feet from us. His jaw drops, and we stand there in silent reverence, knowing this is a moment that must be observed and treated with proper respect.

"SKKXTT! I just saw a flash on the stairs. I'm going up. Over."

"Security! Go! Go! Go!" I shove past Hector and take the lead. But after about a hundred more steps, we're both winded and have to stop on a landing to rest. I think the rent-a-cop chasing us may be more out of shape than we are because his footsteps have slowed way down. It sounds less like a guy chasing somebody and more like my dad on his way up to bed at night. We can rest for a minute. Hector's forehead is dripping sweat down through the metal grate of the landing and onto a huge electrical panel below. Not a great idea. I look around and spot a rag hanging on a nail, so I grab it and give it to Hector so he can wipe his face off. That's when I notice the big red button labeled

Now let me just say that I am not usually this impulsive, but adrenaline has made me do some crazy things

that I can't really explain later when my parents ask me things like,

Maybe some things are just better left unexplored.

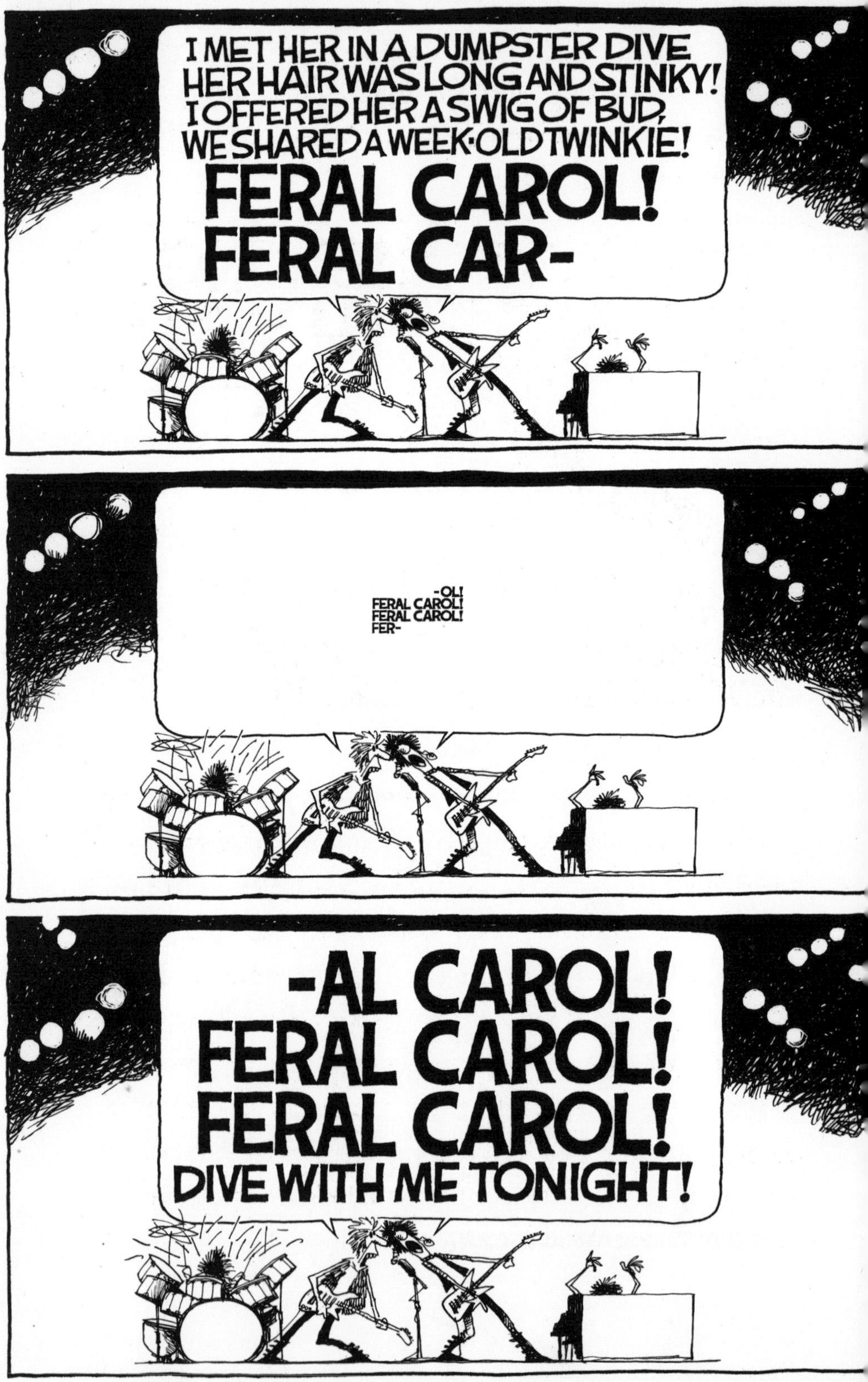
I MET HER IN A DUMPSTER DIVE
HER HAIR WAS LONG AND STINKY!
I OFFERED HER A SWIG OF BUD,
WE SHARED A WEEK-OLD TWINKIE!
FERAL CAROL!
FERAL CAR-
-OL!
FERAL CAROL!
FERAL CAROL!
FER-
-AL CAROL!
FERAL CAROL!
FERAL CAROL!
DIVE WITH ME TONIGHT!

Satisfying . . . very satisfying. After I hit the button a second time and turn the sound back on, I briefly wonder if there is something wrong with me.

THERE IS SOMETHING WRONG WITH YOU!

Suspicion confirmed. Then Hector yells about how we're probably going to die for this, shoves me aside, and gallops up the stairs three at a time. It occurs to me that he could have a point, and so I charge after him. When I hit the top step and duck around a tower of metal beams and braces, a wall of white light blinds me and I crash into Hector. We tumble forward in a heap onto a metal walkway. It takes me a moment to adjust my eyes, but as things come back into focus I realize we are looking over the edge of a catwalk thirty feet in the air, directly above the greatest guitar mayhem band in the world. And they're actually looking back at us.

No! Way! I mean, it's beyond awesome that we're actually backstage—okay, *above* stage—at a Gingivitis concert, but the guys are encoring with their opening number,

"Quintuple Amputee"! I guess it's true that after all these years they can only remember eighteen songs (not so bad . . . these guys have to be in their thirties).

This is my chance. I tell Hector to hold steady, so he hooks his knees onto the guardrail and grabs a handful of denim.

I'm close enough to the band to see the bald spots on the tops of their heads as I zoom in on Nigel's guitar. Ewan is yelling something to a tattoo-faced roadie, who is pointing up at me and yelling at a security guy, who is yelling into his walkie-talkie. I can hear footsteps pounding on the metal stairway over the chorus of the song, but I stay focused and wait. I am going to see how he fingers this chord if it kills me. And Hector. Sorry, dude, but what are friends for?

"We gotta go!" yells Hector.

"One more second," I say, sliding my phone from Camera to Video. Nigel scowls at me and I hit Record.

"Dude! His pinky is on the *seventeenth* fret!"

"Fascinating!" he hollers. "But we gotta go!" I look over and see three huge security guys chugging across the catwalk.

Hector yanks me up and we take off down the other set of stairs.

The crowd noise gets even louder as we hit the floor, so I figure the concert must be over. Hector points off toward the corner of the stage and we can actually see the band being guided off by stagehands carrying tiny flashlights. All at once an old guy in a security shirt pops up from behind a bunch of instrument crates and blocks our way, so we dive under a curtain. The guy's got a good-size gut on him and there's no way he can follow us. All we hear from his side of the partition is "Get back here, you little %$#@!!&*%$#s!" Whoa. Notable expletive. I have so much to learn about the music business.

Fortunately, Hector and I are both dressed in black, so we kind of blend in back here, especially with the food service people, who are also a little sweaty and look like they've been chased for a while. Some guy hands each of us a tray of snacks and snarls,

We're in! I find a roll of white gaffers tape, a Sharpie, and some string, and thanks to some hand lettering (seven years of straight As in art finally pays off big!), our school IDs, and the dim light back here, I make two passable backstage badges that should get us by. There's a big crowd to our right, and using my acute knowledge of rock culture, I conclude that Gingivitis is holding an autograph session.

Nobody budges. We'd have a better chance getting through the Pittsburgh Steelers' defensive line. Then the crowd shifts and starts moving like one big organism toward another room. They must be following the band, but it's impossible to tell what's happening. Then all of a sudden I have two trays of stuffed mushrooms in my hands and I feel myself rising off the floor.

That's more like it! I can see everything! Unfortunately, everybody can see me, including a security guy who recognizes me and yells, "Hey! Skinny kid in black!" That attracts the attention of around seventy other skinny kids dressed in black, and gives me the chance to jump off Hector's shoulders and burrow deeper into the crowd. Actually, this is better because I can look between all the legs and see what's going on, which is really not much.

Everybody cheers when Nigel and Ewan pour rum into a chocolate fountain and light it on fire, but the flames barely reach the ceiling and nothing explodes. Then they just toss their guitars at some roadies and slip through a door to somewhere outside. Show's over, folks.

This is our last chance. I can feel the crowd start to loosen up and go in different directions, so I act. I get behind Hector and yell "PUSH!" and he takes off with me in his slipstream. We spill onto the loading dock into the cold night air just in time to get splattered with beer from a can tossed by a guy as he boards a rusty blue bus. The door slams and the rig rumbles across the parking lot and into the night, leaving nothing but a cloud of diesel smoke and our broken dreams. Just then we hear the distant voice of an announcer saying "Gingivitis has left the building!"

I take the key chain out of my pocket and it falls apart in my hand. A lot of cancer this is going to cure.

CHAPTER 11

"D on't turn around," says Hector.

"I already saw it," I say, as I wring the muddy water out of my sock for the third time. It rained just enough during the concert to fill every invisible pothole in this crummy neighborhood for me to step in while walking back to the van. "Fortunately, I'm immune to irony. Just ask my mom."

I jam my foot back into my wet shoe with a squishy, farty sound that echoes the mood perfectly. I'm done. Hector is done. Mission Unaccomplished. And now we have to tell our parents and friends that all our intentions and efforts netted us a carnival-quality souvenir key chain for a buddy who's trying to save his mom's life. A key chain that will never get used because a) it's broken, and b) I suddenly remember that Tim's moped doesn't even have a key. The evening just keeps getting better and better.

Hector and I lower ourselves into the front seat, which is also wet. Thanks again, rain! We slowly unhook the bungee cord door lock system, then Hector pulls the retainer out of his mouth and slides out the passenger door. I hear a small splash, followed by what is probably some high-octane Spanish cursing.

"I dropped my retainer in the water," he says, sticking his head in the window. "Remind me to rinse it off later."

"Will do," I lie, and he disappears again.

Ten seconds go by and nothing happens. Then ten more. Hector should have gotten the engine going by now, so I turn to look for him and practically smash my nose into his chest.

"My retainer fell apart," he says, "so I can't start the van. Oh, and it looks like the back bumper fell off again."

Caramba, dude.

OBJECTS IN MIRROR MAY BE BIGGER LOSERS THAN THEY APPEAR

"This sucks," I say, muttering the obvious, and reach for my phone. Total Jumbotron humiliation in front of thousands, no jacket or autograph for Tim, and this stupid, bumperless van won't start. If it weren't for almost getting arrested by event security and seeing the most awesome concert in the history of man, this night would be a total waste. I mash the Home button over and over, but my phone screen stays black. *Caramba grande.* All those texts Sara sent me earlier froze my phone and drained the battery.

"Let me see your phone," I tell Hector.

"Yeah, um, mine's dead, too. I got some of my grandma's habanero sauce on it at the snack bar and it fried the SIM card."

"You brought your own hot sauce to a concert?"

"Duh! I can't eat nachos without grandma's hot sauce! The stuff may be highly corrosive to metal and porcelain, but it's really, really good!"

"Which explains why your retainer disintegrated."

"Um, yeah. I guess I forgot to take it out first, so there's that, too."

Okay then. No phones, no money, and we're stranded in a weedy parking lot in a desolate part of town my mom would only drive through with her windows rolled up and her finger on the 911 speed-dial button. That's a really impressive inventory of crapiosity, if you ask me. I go to bang my head on the steering wheel, but I'm interrupted by an unholy screeching sound coming from up the street.

197

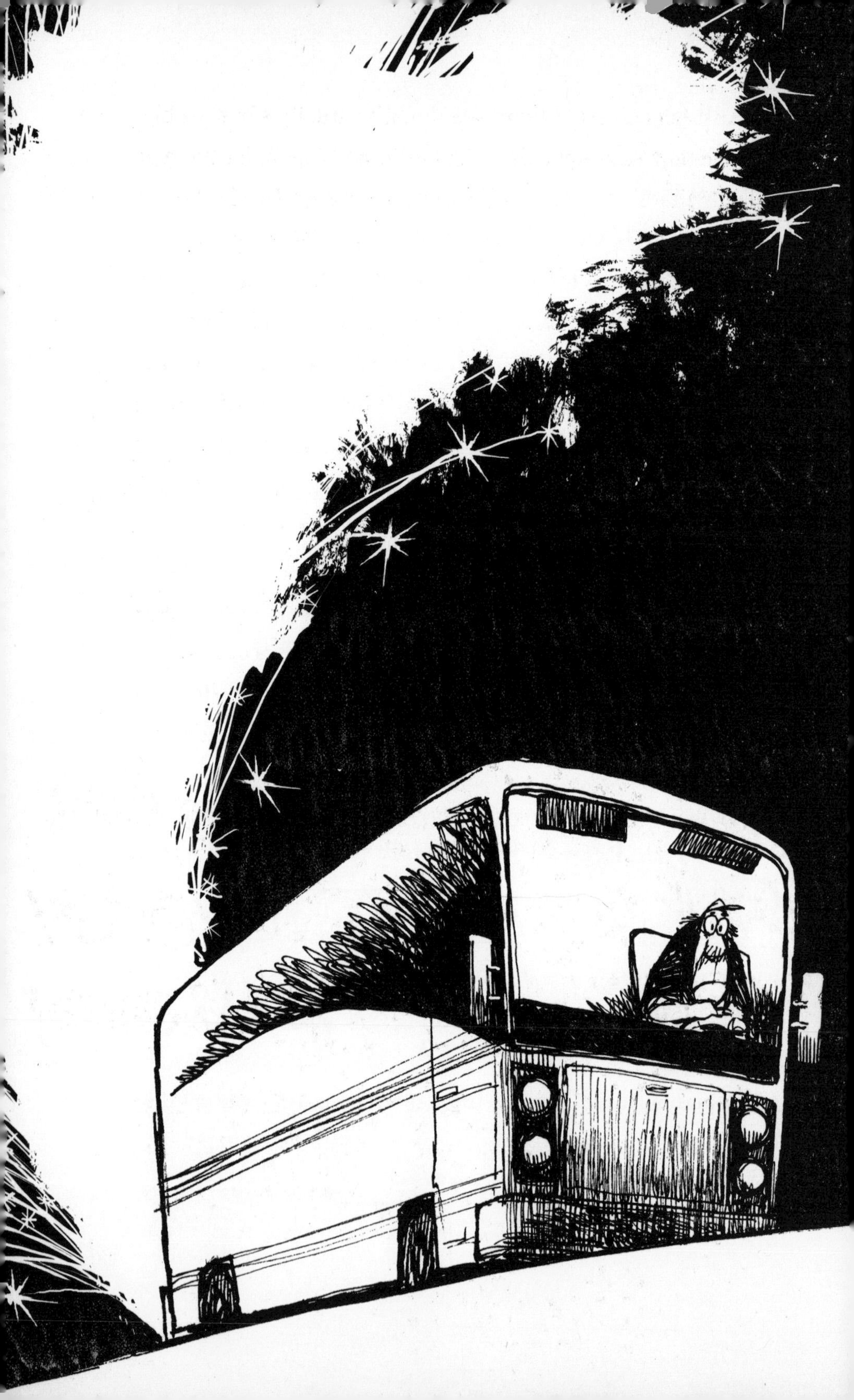

As it gets closer, we can see that it's actually a bus—a big, orange tour bus—and it's dragging something under the rear wheels that's sending sparks up about twenty feet in the air. The driver turns into our parking lot and rolls up to us like a cruise ship docking next to a rowboat. The seamless, glassy finish on the bus gleams in the weird yellow light from the store sign. You wouldn't even know there are windows on the thing except for the woman's leg that's hanging out of an open one near the back. As we're watching, we hear a giggle and the leg kicks a strappy high heel into the air and disappears into the bus. Uproarious laughter. Somebody's living large.

The bus door hisses open and a beer-bellied guy in a black T-shirt with the word *crew* stretched across his chest pounds down the steps and hits the gravel with a thud, accompanied by a chorus of boozy heckling and a tossed beer can. He shuffles toward the back of the bus, muttering something like,

✦★!@.☠︎ℒ⚡︎✗@‼️☮︎⛩️#⚡︎〰︎ⓧ⊘!
⊘★#☄︎%»☠︎🐾000⚒️!🍺🏈★!
☮︎⛩️#〰︎ⓧ⊘!%☠︎★!⅋⊙#◎!

Impressive. Look, I've heard, said, or thought most of those words myself, but I never thought to string them together in one long sentencelike rant. Actually, it would make a great song title. The guy grunts and winces as he kneels down on the jagged asphalt to check under the wheels.

GOOD THING WE'VE GOT A DESIGNATED FLUNKY!

A minute later he's followed by two more burly guys, and Hector punches me hard in the arm.

"Dude! That's the roadie we saw backstage! I recognize his tattoo!" he says.

"Calm down," I say. "A lot of people have tattoos of snakes slithering through the eye sockets of skulls."

"On their foreheads? I don't think so, man! This must be the Gingivitis bus! I bet the crummy blue one we saw leave the arena belongs to the opening act!"

"They sucked, so it follows that their ride should suck, too," I wisely observe. Then we slip out of the van and inch closer so we can hear what they're saying.

And then suddenly everybody is looking at me.

"Hey, skinny kid!" Psycho Forehead Skull Guy yells. "We need a hand." He mutters something else to the others and they all laugh.

I look at Hector, or where Hector was a second ago anyway, and it's pretty clear they mean me. I consider bolting but realize it's, like, thirty blocks of industrial wasteland to the next pay phone, so I gulp, do the "Who, me?"

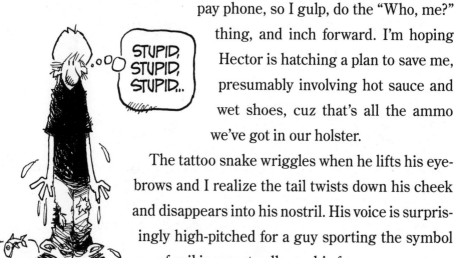

thing, and inch forward. I'm hoping Hector is hatching a plan to save me, presumably involving hot sauce and wet shoes, cuz that's all the ammo we've got in our holster.

The tattoo snake wriggles when he lifts his eyebrows and I realize the tail twists down his cheek and disappears into his nostril. His voice is surprisingly high-pitched for a guy sporting the symbol of evil incarnate all over his face.

"But—these are my good clothes!" I squeak, and then look down at myself. Wrong excuse.

One of my mottoes in life is—and I don't just mean in this particular situation—"Never talk back to a man with a reptile up his nose," so I get on the ground and start squirming under the bus. It's dark and greasy under there, but I feel around and finally get my hand on the chunk of metal. It's lodged in there tight, so I yell, "It won't come loose!"

"Grab it with both hands," one of them says. Then a second later, "You got it?"

"Yeah, but I—" and suddenly they yank me by the ankles and I come scraping on my belly from under the bus holding the problem.

"That would be us," I say, raising a scraped arm. I look around and see that I'm alone. "I mean, me." Then we hear,

What is this, some kind of cursing roadie glee club or something? Everybody's got the same lyrics. I squint through the dim light and see what looks like a cloud of blue smoke with four skinny legs crashing down the steps of the bus. Backlit by the headlights, two figures emerge from the cloud of smoke, walking (well, stumbling really) toward me in slow motion, like one of those corny promo teasers for *Monday Night Football*. I swear that I hear angels singing, until I realize that's just the girl in the bus whining about wanting someone to heat up her crab melt.

And then Nigel Mealsworth and Ewan Ipswich are standing (okay, *swaying*), like, three feet away from me. Seriously, I'm close enough to Gingivitis that I could touch them.

"Cor blimey! Now you've made a hash of it, mates!" yells Nigel, meaning something, I'm sure. Whatever it is, I don't think he's happy because he peels off his leather jacket and slams it to the ground, almost falling over with the effort. A drum cymbal rolls down the steps and shimmers to a stop. Ewan grips a jar of red M&M's to his chest and squints at us through the haze of smoke surrounding his head. I gotta say, these guys look a lot less rock-starish up close than they do from a thousand feet away. Without the hair, I don't think either of them would cast a shadow in bright sunlight. And they sure wouldn't last any longer in a PE dodgeball game than I do. Nigel takes a drag off his cigarette and points at me.

"Yeah," says the driver, kicking the van's bumper around in a lazy circle. "And he just pulled this hunk of junk out of the axle for us." Nigel bends down and glares at the bumper.

"Wot kind of moron leaves somethin' like this in the road for somebody to run over? Whatever 'appened to common courtesy and good citizenship," he yells as he tosses his cigarette into a nearby trash can, which immediately erupts in flames. The trash can fire illuminates the van with its missing bumper, grinning like a third grader with no front teeth. Hector is standing there next to it and gives a little lady wave with his fingers.

Nigel leans over and lights another cigarette (and a little of his hair) off the trash can fire, and I get a better look at his face. Dude, I have seen Google maps with fewer lines. How old *is* this guy? He shuffles over and leans his face close to mine. I hold my breath, mentally calculating the flammability of whiskey breath in the presence of a lit cigarette.

"So you saved our precious bus, then? I suppose thanks would be in order."

"Um, okay. I mean, you're welcome," I finally squeak.

"Really welcome," says Hector. "You guys are our role models." His sentence is punctuated with the other strappy high heel arching through the air and bouncing to a stop at his feet. It's followed by some sort of frilly fishnet stocking that, I notice, matches the bandana in Ewan's hair. Hector turns the color of his grandma's enchilada sauce. Ewan looks at Nigel and shrugs.

"Um, yeah. We have a band and we play a lot of music."

"You don't say," Nigel says, smiling. "Musicians who play music. What do you think 'bout that, Ewan? Very unusual, wouldn't you say?" Ewan cackles and mumbles a string of word-sounding stuff, then cackles again. Now, I know that I'm talking to Nigel Mealsworth, an actual rock star, and that this should be the most amazing moment in my life, but for some reason all I can do is stare at the chasms between the guy's teeth. I guess it comes with being the son of an orthodontist, and I silently curse my frozen phone because my dad would kill for a close-up of this mouth.

"So I guess you think we owe you a big wet kiss on the mouth for fixin' our bus problem, mate. But then, come to that, the bumper from your old beater caused it now, didn't it?" he snarls. "Quite a night's work for a busy li'l kangaroo, eh, Ewan?" and they start hopping toward the bus door, laughing.

"Wait a minute!" I hear some pissed-off person shout using my mouth. "I, um, yeah, I guess I've screwed up my share, but, you know, you've also pretty much YouTubed my life to hell

tonight! You might show a fellow musician enough respect to answer a question!"

Nigel and Ewan stop in their tracks, slowly turn around, and saunter back toward Hector and me. The whole crew is stone quiet. Nigel and I regard each other in silence for the better part of an eternity. Someone should be recording this.

"Well then?"

"I've been working on 'Quintuple Amputee,'" I say. "You know, with the weird chord that nobody but you knows how to play."

"That's bloody ambitious of you," he says, rubbing his skinny arms. It's getting a little cold out here, and the mewling from the girls inside the bus is getting louder. It's not often that you get the full and complete 15 percent of a rock star's attention, so I decide to go for it.

"So, I got a picture of you playing it during the concert, but I just need to be sure . . ." and I stretch my hand out in the chord shape, wiggling my pinky, ". . . it's the seventeenth

fret, right?" Ewan spews a mouthful of whatever he's drinking across the pavement and stumbles around in a circular laughing/coughing fit. Nigel's jack-o'-lantern grin drops about one degree at the corners, and my eyes lock in on what's left of his pupils.

"Ah! Well, let me think now . . ." Ewan has pulled enough oxygen back into his lungs to stand nearly upright again. He takes a couple of steps toward the bus, stoops to pick up the cymbal that rolled out earlier, and hurls himself up the stairs. A second later the big diesel engine rumbles to life, and Nigel says with a kind of a sneer, "Aw, bad luck! The bus is leaving, mate!"

Hector and I turn our backs against the blast of diesel smoke, gravel, and a hail of red M&M's as the bus roars away.

NEXT TIME, EH?

When the smoke clears, we look around. The parking lot looks like the school quad after lunch hour, and these guys were only here for about ten minutes! Two rock stars equals the debris-creating power of an eight-hundred-person student body. Awesome! I kick a mostly empty beer can and send it spinning across the pavement, coming to rest against a lump of something on the ground.

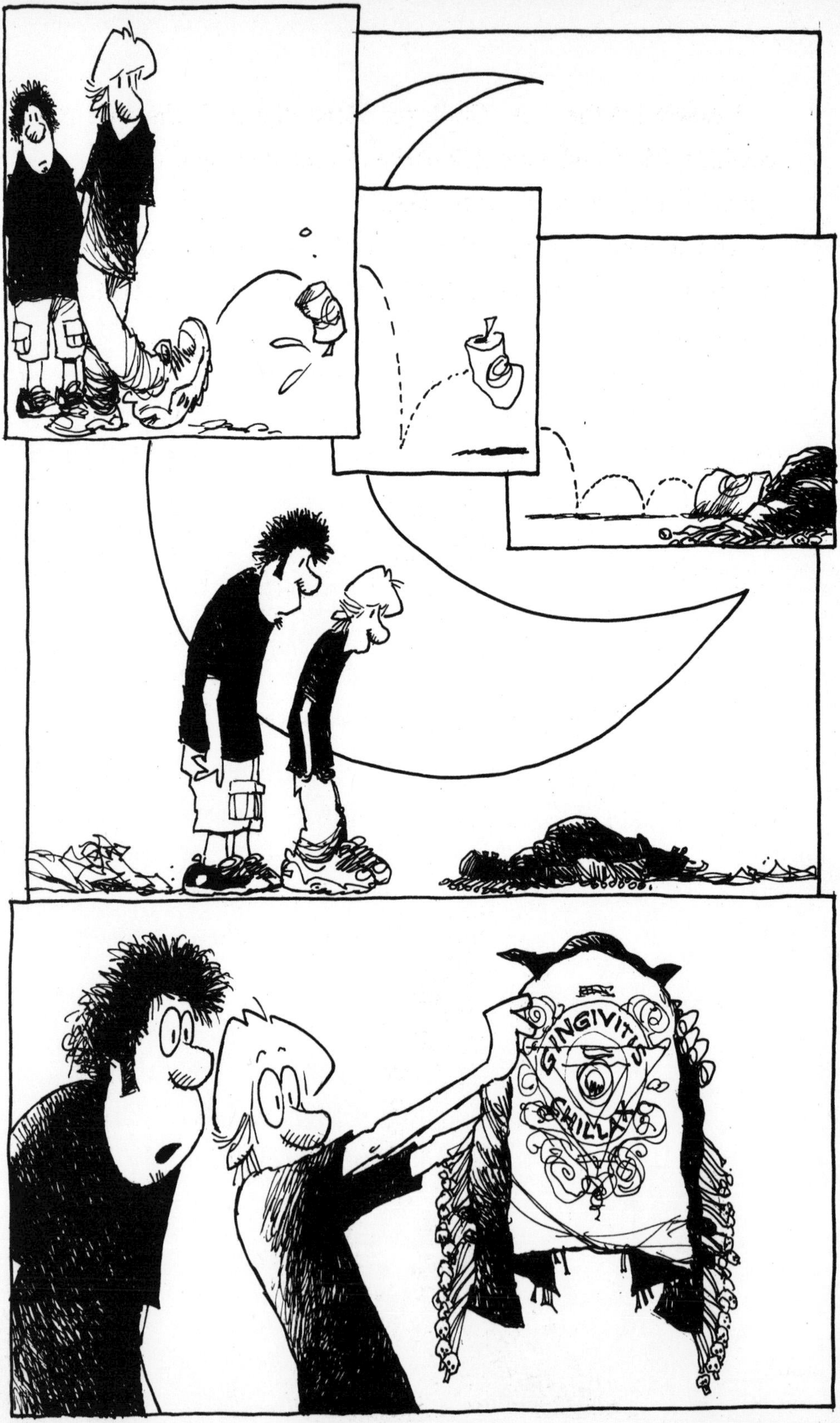
GINGIVITIS
CHILLA

I slowly lift the Holy Grail; the Hope diamond; the split cowhide, fringed-sleeved Ark of the Covenant of Rock 'n' Roll, Nigel Mealsworth's personal jacket.

The taillights of Gingivitis's bus are fading in the distance, but we both know that we really should do something. So I call out to them.

And then everything is quiet. Gingivitis is gone. The trash can fire is out. And Hector and I are holding not a lousy thirty-five dollar souvenir, not even a lousy seven hundred and fifty dollar souvenir, but the garment that once warmed the bony shoulders of an actual rock god. It smells like cigarettes and small regrets, which, come to think of it, would make a killer song title.

"Try it on," Hector whispers. I slip my arm into a sleeve, and a shiver runs up my spine, partly because it's Nigel's jacket, and partly because of the wet Kleenex I find waiting inside the cuff. It helicopters to the ground and we stare at it for a while. "My grandma keeps tissues there, too," Hector says. He nudges the celebrity snot rag with the toe of his shoe. "I bet we could sell this on eBay." But I'm not listening anymore because my hands are exploring the side pockets in the jacket.

Cough drops, Tums, a Hello Kitty coin purse (Who knew?), lyrics scribbled on some panties, and a bottle of the same laxatives I've seen in my parents' medicine cabinet. And then,

in the other pocket, my left hand feels a bunch of small, thin, and triangular things. No. Way.

"Let me see! Let me see," and Hector grabs one from me.
"It's awesome! It's so thin and triangular and plastic and . . .
wait a minute! This is the same crappy pick that we use but
with a Nigel Mealsworth logo stamped on it!"

He's right. I pull one of our picks out of my jeans pocket and
hold them up side by side. They're identical, except for the
logo, which is so cheesy that part of it flakes off in my fingers.
I look back at Hector.

"Gingivitis uses the same crappy picks that we do?"

"No! I mean, yes, but that's not the point," I explain. "The
point is that these are Gingivitis picks, man! Don't you get it?
We don't suck because we have lousy equipment! We suck just
because we suck!"

"Liberating thought, dude. So you're saying that the main difference between our band and theirs is about thirty years of practice and some significant liver abuse," Hector says, and then does a perfect imitation of Ewan's cackle laugh and we both crack up. Hector picks up our bumper, tosses it into the van, and says,

I climb in the driver's seat and go through all the usual steps.

Nothing is happening, so I go around to the back of the van

to see if I can help, and I see that Hector has twisted the pieces of Tim's busted key chain back together. He reaches into the engine compartment and holding the key chain up he says, "Formerly for Tim."

There is a small flash, an electric snapping sound, and then the engine groans to life, as if from a deep coma.

"I'll drive," Hector says, as a puff of smoke floats out of his ear.

"Shotgun," I add unnecessarily, and Hector rolls his eyes.

He adjusts the seat way back, and I notice that the van is
running really good. I pull Tim's new jacket off and
fold it over the seat. With the little silver skulls
on the ends of the fringe grinning back
at me, I crank up the iPod, and
we roll across the parking
lot and toward home.

THE TAXMAN TOOK AN ARM AND A LEG
THE BANKERMAN TOOK THE REST!
GUESS YOU COULD SAY I CAME OUT A HEAD
WITH MY MAN PARTS STILL POSSESSED!
I WON'T BE A QUINTUPLE AMPUTEE!
NO, I WON'T BE A QUINTUPLE AMPUTEE!
I WON'T BE A QUINTUPLE AMPUTEE!
NO, I WON'T BE A QUINTUPLE AMPUTEE!
I WON'T BE A QUINTUPLE AMPUTEE!
I WON'T BE A QUINTUPLE AMPUTEE!
I WON'T BE A QUINTUPLE AMPU

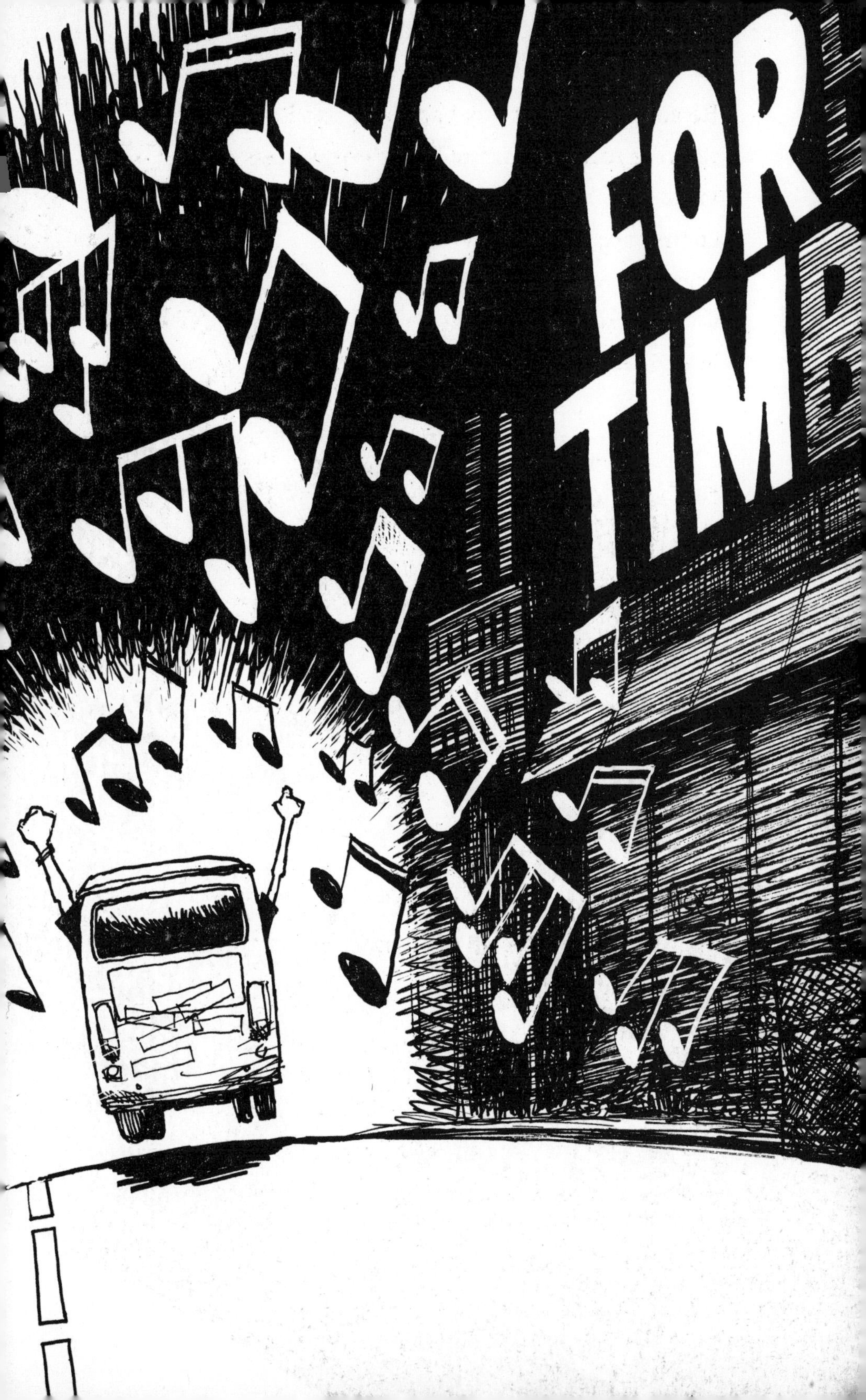
FOR
TIM

CHAPTER 12

The afternoon sun is streaming in the streaky classroom windows, ricocheting tiny dots of light off Ms. Byczykowski's gold crowns. They skate across the classroom walls as she drones details of Civil War battles that are even older than my parents. It's boring, but if you look at it right, it's also like our own little American History disco ball. I'm in a pretty good mood, partly because it's Friday and partly because the band is practicing for the first time under our new name. Chickenfist is no more.

I'm taking credit for coming up with the new band name, which came to me when Hector, Pierce, and I were over at Tim's house a couple of weeks after the bone marrow thing. We were waiting for pizzas to be delivered when the UPS guy came to the door with this box from Tim's uncle in Vermont. Since this was the guy who gave Tim his first guitar and amp, we figured it was more music equipment and tore the box open before the UPS guy was even out the door.

IT SMELLS LIKE GOAT CHEESE.

IT IS GOAT CHEESE.

ARE YOU ON GOOD TERMS WITH THIS UNCLE?

About that time, Taylor from Pizza Guy showed up, all apologetic and carrying three cold pies. Taylor was my supervisor when I worked there last summer. Since pizza season was over, he was back on deliveries full-time and none too happy about it. He's kind of a turd, but I acted like I was glad to see him.

When Taylor started apologizing for the slight (yeah, right) delay, I helpfully pointed out that the unpublished Pizza Guy policy states that if the pizzas arrive more than thirty minutes after the order is placed or if the pizzas are not piping hot (that's the company term for anything warmer than body temperature), he's supposed to give them to us for free.

FREE PIZZA? SERIOUSLY?

Taylor thanked me with eyes as cold and hollow as the black olives stuck to the lid of our pizza boxes, then shrugged and walked out the door. We were all feeling pretty good about the free pizza, so we decided to play a few rounds of Hector's Revenge. The game works like this: One at a time, each person is allowed to put one bizarre topping on Hector's slice of pizza, and then Hector has to taste it. If he pronounces it edible, then everybody has to add the same topping to his own slice and take a bite. It goes on like that until Hector can't choke down a bite of, say, pepperoni/donut hole/tuna fish/Cap'n Crunch/wasabi/sour gummy worm pizza, or we run out of toppings.

We've always run out of toppings.

Anyway, I was up first, so I looked around and spotted the wheel of goat stank from Tim's uncle.

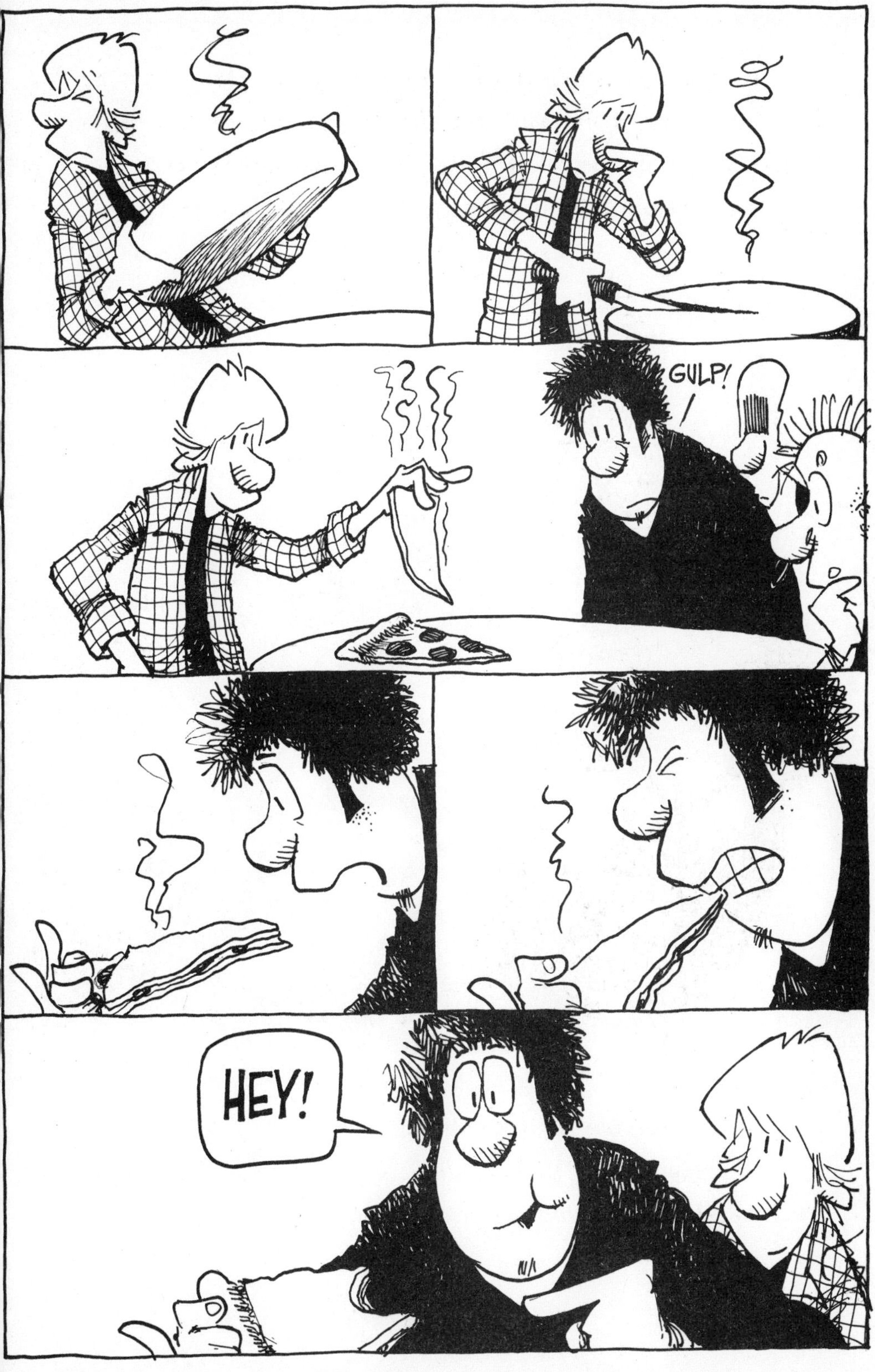
GULP!
HEY!

We were all pretty amazed how something that really stinks could end up being so tasty once we just gave it a chance. Hector pointed out that people usually react the same way to our music, so we changed the name of the band. We are now and forever more:

Ms. Byczykowski stops midsentence, then sighs and closes her lesson book.

"Even I can't pretend this stuff is interesting on a Friday

afternoon. Everybody just take the last few minutes to relax. Please don't leave the room before the bell sounds." A huge cheer goes up from the class and for the last two minutes of class, the air is filled with excited conversation and the muted slapping of thumbs on glass, tapping out overdue texts. Ms. Bycz walks over to Tim, who is still accepting gushing compliments from people on the Gingivitis jacket, which he hasn't taken off since we gave it to him.

She curls her fingers around some of the fringe and nods appreciatively. Then she looks over at me, and something—I don't know . . . some kind of mental high-five, I guess—passes between us.

When the bell finally rings, Tim and I hang back and let everybody else roll through the hallways. His locker is upstairs, too, and neither of us feels like swimming against that current today. We haven't said much for a few days, so I walk over and sit in the desk next to his.

"Yo."

"Yo back," he answers. He is resting one arm on the desk and carefully arranging each of the little silver skulls that are attached to the ends of the sleeve fringe in pairs facing each other, like they're having conversations. "Have I told you how awesome this jacket is?"

"I have no idea what we were thinking when we gave it to you, dude," I said. "We are total chuckleheads. I checked out a YouTube video where Nigel is hugging Mila Kunis wearing that very jacket. Those rivets have been one extremely thin silk blouse away from her naked body."

Tim reverently touches one and closes his eyes. For a moment he's swept far, far away, and then he shudders back and looks around to see if anybody saw that. Okay, AWK-WARD. But it's cool. We've been through worse. And by "we" I mean "he."

When I got home from the Gingivitis concert that night I couldn't sleep. Around 4 a.m. I finally watched the bone marrow donation video my mom had sent me a link to. There's something about imagining your bro lying facedown in an operating room with hypodermic needles sucking juice out of his pelvic bone that makes other stuff look small.

Everything is quiet again while Tim reverses all the skulls into new conversation pairs.

"So during that procedure, do you think all the nurses were looking at your hairy butt the whole time?" I ask sensitively.

Tim snorts. "Dude, I hope not. That would have killed their desire for any other man. Besides, I happen to know the rest of me was draped except where they went in."

"Did it hurt? What I mean is, like, you know—did it hurt?"

"Not during. Not as much as I expected. Now it just feels like I rode my bike off a twenty-foot cliff and landed on my left hip. It's not that bad."

"Been there," I say. And then someone using my mouth says, "How are you feeling about all this? I mean, you know, if guys had feelings and all, like, what do you suppose they would be, I mean, if they did?"

My words sort of hang in the air like one of Hector's fajita-night farts, and I'm about to award myself the Girl Question of the Century Prize.

"To be honest . . ." Tim says, and then it's like the air goes out of him and he sinks into the desk. "I'm all over the place. One minute I don't believe it's happening. The next minute I'm saving the world. And the next minute I'm just barely hanging on, trying to keep everything from spinning so fast and flinging me into space. Sometimes I think I just can't do it. But, you know, it's my mom and all. Sitting on the bench while she goes through this is not an option."

"Dude," I say, and I mean it.

"The good part is that my mom is doing better. Her numbers are good, my dad says, and yesterday when I got home she was cutting quilt squares from her fabric, which she hasn't done for forever. It almost felt like old times last night."

"This is more words than I've heard you string together in the two years that I've known you," I say. "I always thought you were just a doofus. I mean, in a good way." We almost fist-bump but we both get creeped out at the same moment and do a sort of elbow slide thing that's just as bad. The final bell announces the end of Sensitivity Hour, and we head over to my house.

Two hours later, Goat Cheese Pizza is tuning up and adjusting mics in my garage. The crowd is huge by our standards—I even had to get the extra blue folding chair from the basement. It's about six degrees off level, but so is P-Mom by this time on most Friday afternoons, so everything is cool.

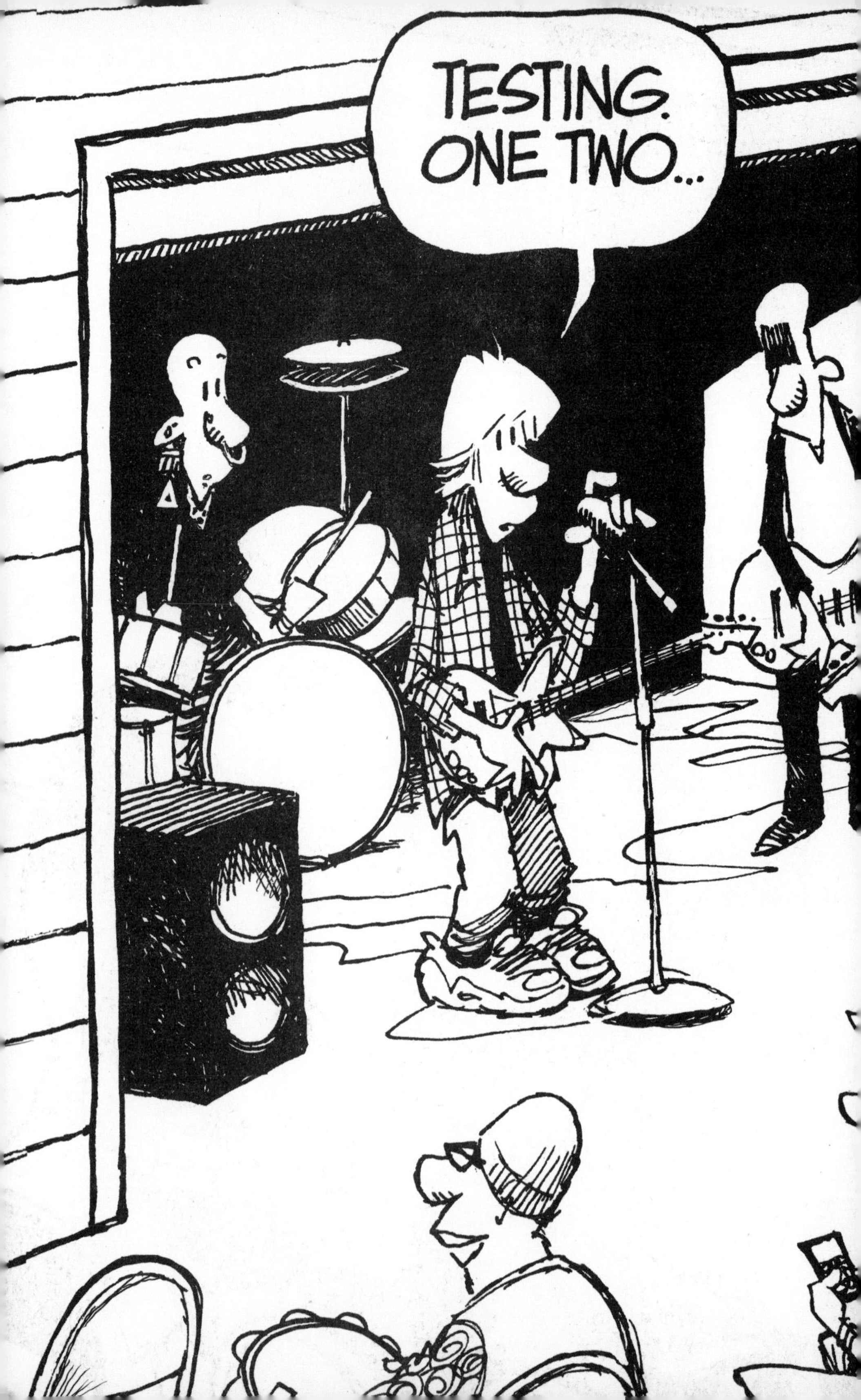
TESTING. ONE TWO...

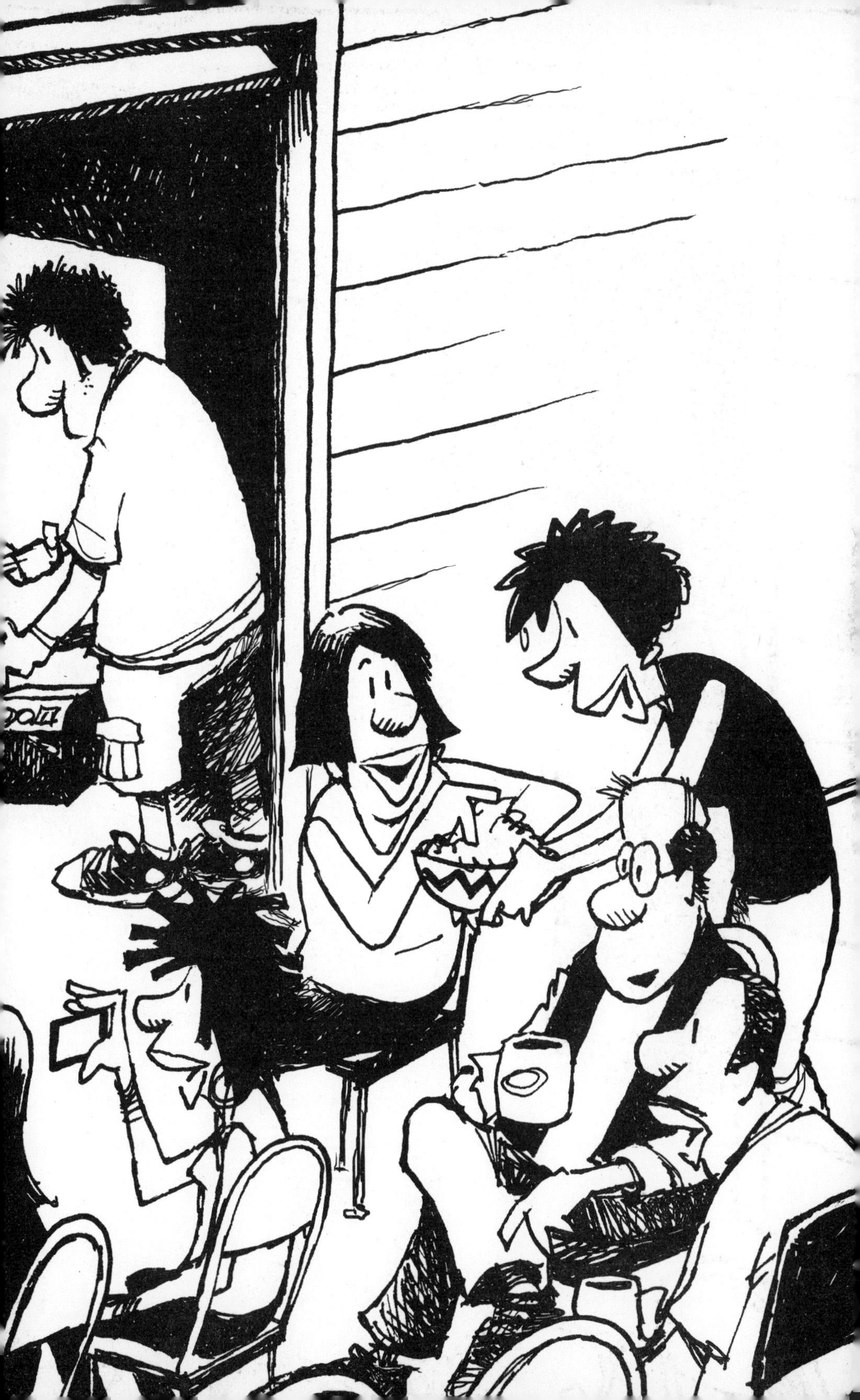

When we see a red Toyota pull up, Tim shoots out of the garage, almost taking out half of Pierce's drum kit in the process. A few seconds later he and his dad are helping T-Mom up the driveway as she holds onto their arms. Everybody is clapping and cheering, and I think my mom may even be crying a little.

We all take turns saying hi and telling her how good she looks, which is true. It's pretty cool. Pierce and P-Mom make their way through the crowd, and P-Mom practically smothers the poor woman with new age healing hugs and affirmations. After absorbing about all the positive energy one person can possibly stand, T-Mom says, "Oh. I have something to show you . . ."

...SURPRISE!

It turns out that she never did lose her hair, a minor detail that Tim failed to mention. But it's all good. Pierce and his mom think the whole thing is hilarious and immediately update their Facebook pages with pictures of their heads bookending T-Mom's grinning face, like a couple of albino bowling balls.

"How's the new ignition switch working, guys?" I look up at Hector's dad and my dad wading through the cables, foot pedals, and sound equipment that they've financed over the years.

"Good," says Hector.

"Yeah. It's really cool," I add. "And the interior hardly even smells like scorched hair anymore." A few days after the concert Hector's dad decided that it would be a lot cheaper for him to fix the van's starting problem than to keep buying new retainers. My dad steps up onto Pierce's riser and motions Hector over.

"Let's have a look," he says, and Hector opens his mouth. "Hm. Good."

The wonky output jack on my guitar must be loose again because I feel all tingly on one side. I unplug, but it doesn't go away. Then I realize that the electric current running down my arm is all about the Sara connection and not the instrument.

I give her my best genuine-but-not-too-genuine-or-goofy-bad-boy-rock-god smile, and she melts away. Digging into my front pocket, my fingers touch triangular inspiration. I look back at Pierce and he counts off the beat for "Quintuple Amputee." Since I play lead on this tune, the guys sail into the intro while I take a couple of seconds to stare at the Nigel Mealsworth signature cheapo official Chillax Tour nylon guitar pick pinched between my fingers. It's weird. I've carried this thing around with me like a talisman since it was exhumed from Nigel's jacket pocket, but I've never actually played a guitar with it. Maybe this is the moment. Maybe this is the magic. Maybe tonight I'll get the insanely difficult chord right for once, which I think is totally possible because— Wait. Why did the music stop?

DUDE!

"Would you care to join us in playing this selection?" Hector asks. Then everybody laughs.

"Very funny. I was, uh, thinking about something else. Let's go again . . . Hunh! Hoo! Hree! Faw!"

This time I'm into it; we actually sound pretty good for a change. The old license plates nailed to the wall behind Pierce rattle crazily on their nails, shuddering in time with Tim's bass line and Sara's hips. My fingers stretch out, searching for the chord. I squeeze my eyes shut, reach my pinkie down toward the seventeenth fret, and—

I nail it-ish. I look over at Tim and he raises an eyebrow and nods. I know it doesn't seem like much, but for him it's the enthusiasm equivalent of a naked double backflip. Hector and Tim lean in to the mic and start the opening chorus, and I can tell by the look on their faces that, minus the pyrotechnics, hair, bad teeth, and compromised liver function, we look and sound pretty authentic. Not perfect, but close. And, as it turns out, close is close enough for now.

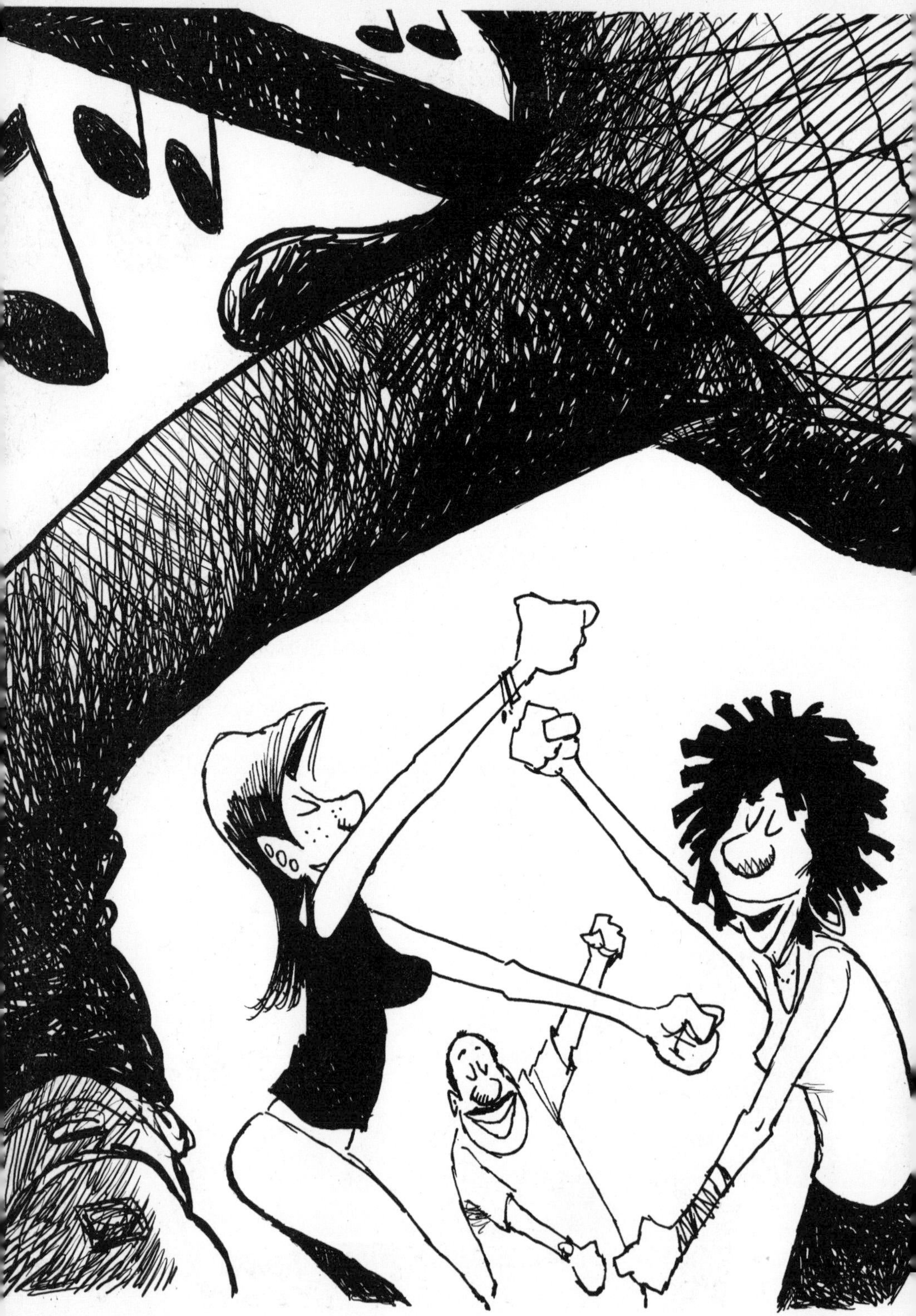

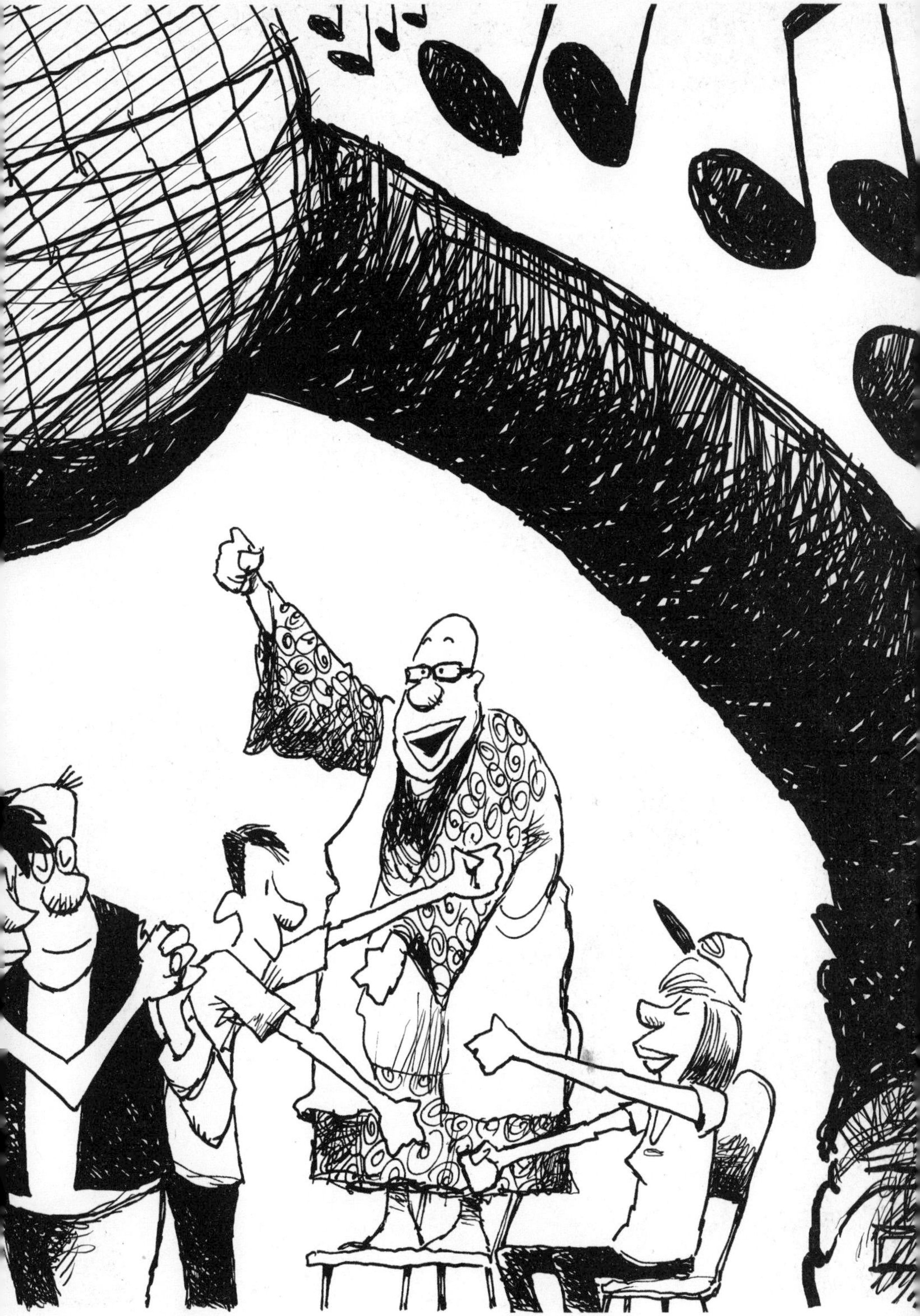

Check out even more TOTALLY AWESOME stuff
for Jeremy and the gang in

ZITS: SHREDDED!

A sneak peek is next . . . WHOA!

That's the trouble with milking french fries—slippery elbows. Once you've been at it for a couple of hours you get grease slicks down your forearms that threaten your stability. One careless bump from, say, your 230-pound sumo-size best friend and you can go skidding forward across the table, sending a giant cup of your morning's work sliding ahead of you. As in just now. We all freeze as the oily Big Slurp teeters on the edge and then dumps about seventeen fossil fuel–free miles onto the floor and into the crisp cuffs of some salesman's khakis.

2

Ever since we had the van converted to run on veggie oil, Hector, Pierce, and I have been scrounging stray fries and orphan onion rings off abandoned fast-food trays and squeezing the free mileage out of them. It's annoyingly slow, and even if we're careful we can't get more than a cup of grease out of a small order of fries. There are sixteen cups in a gallon, and the van has a ten-gallon tank. Do the math. There's no way I'm wasting this puddle of liquid freedom.

"Don't just sit there," I yell. "SCOOP!" Pierce dives for the floor, and Hector grabs a spare cup while I try to surround the pool of oil that's spreading slowly across the table.

Before long, we salvage most of the spill, and I carefully snap a plastic lid on the cup. Out of the corner of my eye, I see the salesman guy flipping us off on his way out the door.

"What's his problem?" I ask.

"No idea," says Pierce. "Dude was slapping at me with the comics section the whole time I was under his table. Talk about anger issues!"

Hector scrolls through the apps on his phone and then taps the maps icon. He sits up really straight and gets this weird, plastic look on his face.

"Contestants," he rumbles in a deep, corny announcer voice. "The category is: 'Historic Cool Places We Should Visit.'"

"Can we just have a normal conversation for once?" Pierce moans. "As in, *If you were going to get a Renaissance painting tattooed on the roof of your mouth, which one would it be?*'"

Ignoring him, Hector goes on.

"This band famously played a nineteen-hour jam at the Pioneer Inn in Nederland, Colorado, that launched their career. You have five seconds." Then he starts to hum that *Jeopardy* tune. Hector's game-show host imitation always cracks me up. I hate that buzzer of his, though.

"Does anybody have a guess?" Hector prides himself on his

obscure rock trivia, and he totally thinks he has me stumped. I fan the air and raise my hand.

"Who is the String Cheese Incident? Duh. Does anybody not know that?" Hector slumps back down to his normal posture and mumbles something in Spanish. He hates it when I get these answers right.

"AARGH! I knew that one," Pierce howls and then pops a mutant onion ring in his mouth. A half second later he remembers where we found those onion rings.

"Dude! Keep your head in the game! That's free fuel you're wasting," I yell.

"Sorry . . . sorry," he mumbles as he wipes his tongue on his T-shirt, then wrings his T-shirt into the cup. Then we all get back to the business of milking french fries.

Converting the van to run on veggie oil has been kind of a hassle, to tell you the truth. It all started when Sara came back from an OSSWRAC (Overly Strident Students World Resource Austerity Conference) in Columbus last fall. She was all hyped up about stuff like eliminating fossil fuels and stopping global

5

warming. I was picking her up after band practice when out of nowhere she gets this amazing idea:

Who knows what inspires these insights? At the time, it seemed like an awesomely excellent suggestion, but let's face it, almost any suggestion is awesomely excellent when the suggester is a hot girl wearing skinny jeans, boots, and a tight tank top. I mentioned it to Hector, who mentioned it to Pierce, who called his uncle, the motorcycle mechanic, who happened to know everything there is to know about converting diesel engines to run on veggie oil. He got his automotive training at an ashram in Bhutan, so he's a master of reincarnated engines. And he knows his yaks, too.

There were a couple of problems to overcome right away,

like the fact that the van didn't have a diesel engine and it was going to cost *way* more than we could afford. But Pierce's mom stepped in and traded Pierce's uncle the bail money he still owed her for the cost of converting the van. We even got to help with the conversion, which we all found educational.

After about a hundred trips to the junkyard and a month of weekends, we actually got the van's new used diesel engine running on recycled veggie oil. And even though it can be kind of a pain to scrounge for used grease, the van is more awesome than ever because (1) it's überly good for the planet (the van's old motor put enough CO_2 in the atmosphere to melt an iceberg),

(2) it's a total chick magnet, and

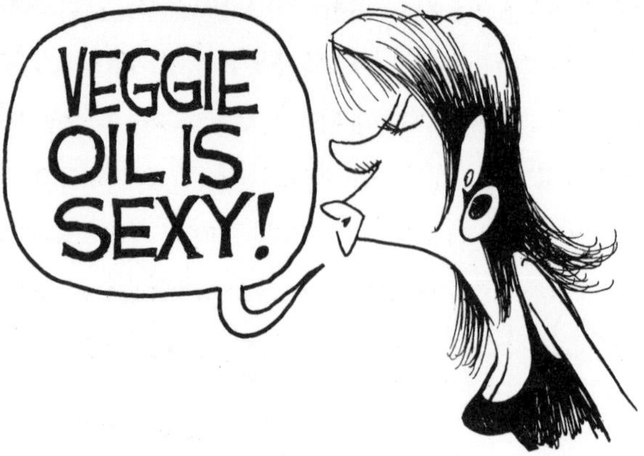
VEGGIE OIL IS SEXY!

(3) it always smells like french fries.

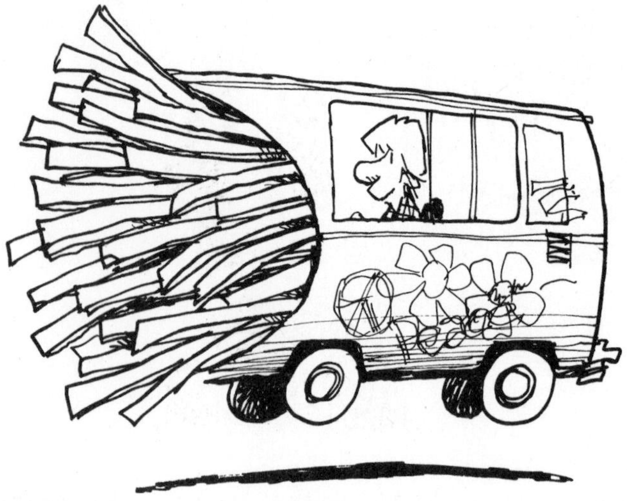

Combine that with the fact that the fuel is basically free and available in any fast-food Dumpster or alley and you have a win-win-win-win situation.

I squeegee another drop of oil into a fresh cup and catch a glimpse of Hector tapping on his phone screen again. We've been working out the route of our Epic Summer Road Trip since we bought the van. The plan is to take off the day after we graduate and spend the summer rolling down the highway on good karma and fast-food squeezings. Yeah, okay, it's still a ways off, but a journey of this magnitude takes serious planning. Hector switches off his calculator app and announces, "At twenty-five miles per gallon, the String Cheese detour to Colorado would take just over forty-nine gallons of grease."

"Totally agree," I say. "Add it to the itinerary." And then we all groan as a big jock at the next table downs two huge fistfuls of fries whose partially hydrogenated innards would have gotten us halfway to St. Louis.

"Let's get back to Midwest destinations," suggests Hector. He holds his phone up for Pierce and me to see. "I think it's pretty clear that there's nothing really interesting between Moline, Illinois (the birthplace of three of the founding members of Flatulent Rat), and Hibbing, Minnesota (the birthplace of Bob Dylan), agreed?"

"Just Chicago." Pierce shrugs.

"Right. So it only makes sense that we'd head west from Hibbing and drive straight through to Jamestown, North Dakota."

"Correct," says Hector. "And the next logical stop would be . . . ?"

"Jerome, Arizona, home of the world's best buffalo-wing restaurant," I answer, channeling his brain.